RANGER'S GAME

The two outlaws sat waiting. Suddenly Hatfield appeared and Meacham turned to smile at him, caught the glint of metal on the man's shirt, and froze . . .

"Ranger!" Meacham gasped.

"You're under arrest," the Ranger said in a steady voice. "Charged with murder, accessory to murder and rustlin'. Coming peaceful?"

The outlaws stared at Hatfield. "All this time," Meacham whispered, "we never knew."

Suddenly Meacham's eyes narrowed and his hands went for his guns. His partner did the same. Hatfield had only a breath of warning . . .

TROUBLE RANGE

Jackson Cole

WILDSIDE PRESS

CHAPTER I

Trouble Range

It had been an hour since Captain William McDowell of the Texas Rangers had clumped into his office at Headquarters in Austin The reports from posts and operators scattered over the great sweep of Texas had elicited only a few muttered growls, and the clerk closed the door with a sigh of relief The mail was heavy but there might not be anything explosive in it.

For half an hour the bright sun streamed in the windows on a peaceful office. Then abruptly McDowell's door was burst open

"Where's Hatfield?" he roared "Get the file on the Brant Trimpe killin' up in Matos! Dig out the AX brand and the syndicate that owns it. Where in blue blazin' cusses is Hatfield!"

His door slammed as the clerks jumped to obey. Grizzled brows drawn in a deep frown, he crossed the office to stand before a big map of Texas His eyes lifted to the Panhandle, spotted Amarillo, then dropped south to Matos, indicated in small type.

"Old buff'lo huntin' country," McDowell muttered, "before Goodnight and some of them others made mighty rich range out of her."

He turned and sat down at his desk Far better than anything printed, the map of Texas was impressed in his memory He had ridden over most of the state, carrying Ranger justice along the danger trails

From the piny forests of the east to the grim desert country west of the Pecos, and deep in the Big Bend his law guns had brought many an outlaw to the hangnoose or Boot Hill He knew the Rio Grande country and the Gulf strip He had trailed into the great unmarked ocean of grass that was the Panhandle.

Advancing age had pinned him to a swivel chair but

his brain was as keen as ever. He could recall each trail he had ridden, each section of the country. As chief of the Texas Rangers now, his memory of those old days was invaluable.

What had happened long ago, however, was not his only value to the state he served. For nothing occurred now that he was not aware of it. If there was a killing in Van Horn or a holdup in Matamoras, McDowell soon knew about it. If a renegade bullet killed a cowboy near Adobe Wells, or rustlers ran off cattle near Marathon, the report came to McDowell's desk.

His pride was Texas, his mission in life to protect its people, and with his fiery disposition of a Southern gentleman, and the touchy pride of the Texan for his beloved state, anything which touched either sent his anger soaring

A clerk came in, hastily dropped two folders on the desk before him. McDowell opened one, quickly getting the gist of it. His fist smacked on the desk, inkwell and tinkle bell jumped. He opened the second folder, and in a matter of minutes had the information about the AX brand spread at his fingertips. He hit the tinkle bell. The door was instantly opened.

"Blast it, where's Hatfield?" McDowell demanded, not looking up from the file.

"I'm here, chief," a quiet voice answered. There was a touch of laughter in the voice but also deep respect and liking for this irascible old man who ruled the Rangers.

McDowell's head jerked up Ranger Jim Hatfield seemed to fill the doorway He stood well over six feet in his spurred and polished half-boots. His level gray-green eyes were glinting now with a quiet humor. McDowell grunted, and his anger lost its fiery glow.

"Come in, Jim, and close the door. Got some more trouble, looks like, up Panhandle way." His face reddened, and his fist hit the desk again "Cuss the gents that think they're smart enough to beat the law to a frazzle! Blast the sidewinders that's always schemin' to steal a neighbor's last cow or foot of range!"

"Better tell me about it, chief," Hatfield said in a lazy drawl, as he slouched into a chair.

6

Jim Hatfield had none of the outward marks of a quick-triggered fighting man. Yet he was the man to whom McDowell gave the hardest jobs, the most puzzling, the most dangerous. And he had yet to fail the grizzled old Ranger chief

He looked to be a good-natured, big cowboy. His fresh laundered blue shirt was topped by a red bandanna, and was tucked into dark trousers His big Stetson had been shoved to the back of his head, revealing jet-black hair that had a youthful sheen as the light struck it His legs were muscular and powerful, and his broad shoulders strained at the shirt seams, but his torso tapered down to narrow hips, from which depended heavy cartridge belts supporting matched blue-steel Colts.

His face, bronzed by the Texas sun, was as angular as though cut from granite The quick smile of his wide lips could swiftly soften his stern, somewhat severe features. His gray-green eyes were keen and alert, revealing the explosive power of the man that was always under control of his analytical, quick-thinking brain. He typified McDowell's own youth, the living symbol of the adventurous, danger-shot days when McDowell himself had ridden the long Texas trails.

"Ever heard of the AX brand?" McDowell asked.

Hatfield frowned, then his eyes cleared.

"Up in the Panhandle, chief. It's a big outfit, as I recall "

Hatfield accepted the letter that McDowell handed across the desk He read it and looked up. McDowell stabbed a gnarled finger at the paper.

"That comes all the way from Liverpool I'd say there's a heap of Injuns in the woodpile up there at the AX. Ain't often these English syndicates worry much about the details like this "

"Rustlin' has been goin' on for a considerable time as shown by the manager's reports," Hatfield said slowly. "There have been some killin's that he blames on farmers who have taken up claims on AX range."

"Like a heap of others," McDowell cut in, "AX grazes more range than it rightfully owns It works all right till some gent files on it and then blue blazes generally pops.

AX has been tryin' to buy up the farm claims peaceful."

Hatfield placed the letter back on the desk and quickly summarized

"But there's plenty of trouble The local law can't handle it The syndicate sent their business man down from Denver to do what he could with the farmers In the mean time, they're askin' us to look into it. What happened to the business manager?"

"He was a gent named Brant Trimpe," McDowell said. "He arrived in Matos a couple of months ago to look things over and parley with the nesters He didn't get far He's dead"

"Murdered?" Hatfield asked, brows raising.

McDowell thumped another report on his desk.

"Law up there said it was plumb accidental This Trimpe gent got mighty careless with a Colt he was cleanin' Blowed the top of his head off about two weeks ago Seems like the ranch manager was plumb sorry but mighty helpless The lawman up there in Matos investigated and made no arrest. Accident, they said "

McDowell snorted and started pacing back and forth before the map. He turned, clasping his gnarled hands behind his back

"Jim, this is a mighty funny case One way yuh look at it, everything's open and aboveboard Farmers come in on open range and file claims. AX tries to buy 'em out, has some trouble and sends Brant Trimpe to smooth things over He kills hisself All the syndicate can do is appoint a new business manager and start over again "

"Except for the rustlin'," Hatfield observed. "That's our job "

"Rustlin's just part of it," McDowell said shortly. "Brant Trimpe might not have killed hisself, no matter what the sheriff says Mebbe the farmers bushwhacked him—or somebody else did Might be the farmers are rustlin' them cows, but it ain't likely Jim, yuh're headin' for Matos "

"Any other ideas, chief, before I start ridin'?" Hatfield asked.

"It's up to you, Jim. Find out how Trimpe really died. Find out who's stealin' them AX cows and doin' the gunslingin' up in Matos. I reckon yuh know yuh're not to leave up there till the range is peaceful and the trouble smashed These English gents thought enough of the glorious state of Texas to invest their money in it They're thinkin' by now we ain't nothin' but a bunch of sidewindin' bushwhackers and rustlers! Why, cuss it, any tarnation son of a spavined mule that blots the fair name of Texas ought to be hung higher'n Haman!"

"Chief," Jim Hatfield cut in with a laugh, "yuh'll plumb bust an artery. I'll head out for Matos right away."

McDowell shook hands with him and sat down at his desk Long after Hatfield had gone, the old man kept muttering under his breath But his anger gradually left him The Matos case was in the capable hands of Ranger Jim Hatfield.

CHAPTER II

Murder Fight

It had been a long ride from the nearest railroad station to Matos Jim Hatfield arrived just as the sun sank below the unbroken sweep of the western horizon He had swung off the train early that morning and had supervised the unloading of his magnificent golden sorrel He had allowed the mount to gallop and roll, race in a huge circle, bucking occasionally to get the kinks of the long train ride out of his back.

When finally Hatfield whistled, the golden horse came galloping straight for him, and nuzzled the caressing hand Hatfield extended. The Ranger slipped on bridle and saddle. A carbine was snugged in a leather boot, and Hatfield's poncho was rolled up at the cantle. Saddle-bags contained extra ammunition and iron rations. With a little salt, sugar and coffee, Hatfield could live indefinitely on the land.

When Hatfield had finished saddling Goldy, the station master, watching, sighed deeply.

"That shore is a fine piece of hoss-flesh, mister," he said. "There's folks in these parts that'd meet any price yuh set on him."

"He ain't for sale," Hatfield drawled, with a friendly smile. He gestured toward a beaten trail that led toward the northern horizon "That the way to Matos?"

"That's it," the man answered. He looked sharply at Hatfield "It's yore business, of course, but stay away from Matos if yuh aim to make a land claim there. There's some figgers the land is all theirs, and they ain't particular how they prove it."

Hatfield's smile was lazy.

"I heard there was ridin' jobs to be had, that's all "

"Then yuh won't have much trouble—unless yuh buck the AX. There's been some killin' up there and some AX

10

cows have disappeared Don't know much about it, but it sounds like yuh might use them sixes yuh wear plumb sudden up Matos way "

"Is the AX a big spread?" Hatfield asked carelessly.

"Mighty big " The man nodded toward the cattle pens across the switch "They ship from here. Not as much as they used to, though, and I don't savvy that. Good graze and a fine strain of beef ought to make 'em plenty of dinero But lately their beef tally to the market has blamed near dropped to half what it was."

"Mebbe they won't need riders then." Hatfield frowned.

The station master glanced at the twin Colts the tall cowboy wore.

"Might be they'd take a fancy to yore hardware," he said slowly.

"Thanks," said Hatfield. He swung into saddle and waved a friendly good-by.

In this land of great spaces, as he rode away toward the north, he could see for miles across the deep grass. At times he had the feeling that he was riding along on the bottom of a gigantic bowl and that the land tipped up all around him to meet the brazen sky. The wide, dusty road had few turnings. There were no fences, and the Ranger saw no sign of human habitation.

In the early days a man had needed a compass to ride across these Staked Plains. The great expanse, like an ocean of grass, had been a barrier to settlers. Only the Indians knew of the water-holes and game trails that were their guides. Time and again men had died out here of hunger and thirst, wandering in great aimless circles.

At last Hatfield, caught sight of two distant ranches, the buildings sharply etched against the sky. Now and then he saw cattle, looking strangely elongated in this flat country.

He saw the town of Matos long before he reached it. At first it appeared to be a series of angular irregularities against the sky, then he could distinguish buildings A few cottonwood trees broke the straight line of the horizon and bushes marked the course of a small stream.

The western sky was a blaze of fiery red and purplish blue when Hatfield rode into Matos' only street. His quick eyes swept over the place as he slouched lazily in the saddle.

Square frame houses raised their gaunt unlovely shapes along the roadway. They gave way to false-fronted buildings A church raised a thin steeple at the far end of the street It had a decrepit look as though the congregation were small and poor A saddle shop and smithy stood on the opposite side of the street.

There were a couple of general stores, an ugly brick bank with offices above it. There were two saloons on opposite sides of the street Lamps began to glow in the windows as the purple coils of night silently writhed into the town Hatfield headed the golden sorrel toward one of the hitch-racks. There were a few horses at the rack as he dismounted and beat the dust of travel from his clothing A loafer silently watched him from the canopied porch of the saloon, his suspicious eyes never shifting from Hatfield's lithe form The Ranger crossed the rickety porch, pushed through the batwings and into the saloon.

Three men stood at the long bar The poker tables were empty, half in shadow A hanging lamp cast a golden circle of light over the bar A bald-headed man with a drooping eyelid swished a dirty cloth over the mahogany His dull eyes swept over Hatfield, but the rag continued its lazy circle.

"Howdy," he said, in a heavy voice "What'll it be?"

"A drink—and some information," Hatfield drawled.

Two of the men turned to stare at him. Both had the tense look, the stubbled faces of outlaws Hatfield noticed that their holsters were carried low for a swift and easy draw

"Here's yore drink," the barkeep said "I ain't so shore about the other. Folks in these parts ain't any too curious "

Hatfield placed a coin on the bar, grinned.

"Neither am I—except to find out if there's a ridin' job in these parts. Heard there's a big spread up this way."

12

"There is." The bartender nodded. "The AX, but I don't know nothin' about if they're hirin'."

One of the gunslingers looked at Hatfield sharply. The golden flecks in the fellow's green eyes made them look wild and dangerous. Lanky black hair escaped from under the dusty gray Stetson on the back of his head. His low forehead was deeply scored by two long wrinkles His lips were unhealthy red in the black stubble on his jaw and upper lip.

"Hoeman?" he asked shortly.

Hatfield looked around. "No. Cowpuncher mostly."

"Gunslinger?" another man asked abruptly.

He stood apart from the others at the far end of the bar. He wore a denim jacket and dirt stained overalls, the usual Texan boots but without spurs. His long face was lined with worry and there was an angry glint in his dark eyes.

"What I am; friend," Hatfield answered easily, "is my own business. I said cowpuncher. Reckon it had better ride that way"

The man's lips twisted and he shrugged work-rounded shoulders.

"Them matched Colts give yuh away. Yuh'll get a job on the AX, all right. They're lookin' for guns."

"Meanin' somethin', Ray?" snapped the gunhawk who had spoken to Hatfield.

"Anyway yuh want it, Lanky Reynolds," the man at the end of the bar answered wearily and pushed his empty glass toward the barkeep. "Another one—to get the smell of wolf out of my nose."

The man he had called Reynolds hitched up his gunbelts, but his companion checked him and rolled his eyes significantly toward Hatfield. The Ranger saw the swift signal but pretended indifference. As he emptied his glass he saw Reynolds rub his hand along his stubbled jaw and shoot a murderous glance at the man he had called Ray. He picked up his glass and came over to Hatfield.

"That's Ray Logsdon," he said in a loud, carrying voice. "One of them blasted hoemen. Where I come from, we got a different name for 'em. Rustlin's bad enough, but bushwhackin' is worse"

Hatfield saw Ray Logsdon's face turn paper-white and his fingers tightened around his glass.

"I never take chips in a game where I don't hold cards, friend," the Ranger said, trying to head off trouble. "But seems like yuh throw words around mighty careless Nobody I see right now fits yore description Mebbe we'd better all have a drink and take a fresh tally"

He gestured to the bald-headed barkeep who filled the four glasses and poured one for himself Logsdon stared at his drink, lips pulled into a thin, tight line Hatfield's sharp eyes traveled over him. The man wore no holster or belt but there was a suspicious bulge in one of the big patch pockets of his denim coat.

"Here's mud in all yore eyes," Hatfield said, with a laugh, but his eyes were sober and sharp. "And to yore town, yore ranchers and yore farmers"

"Didn't leave a thing out," the barkeep marveled. "Luck, friend."

The men beside Hatfield downed their drinks. Logsdon hesitated, then nodded briefly to Hatfield, tossed his down, and pushed away from the bar Reynolds turned swiftly as though to intercept the man, but Logsdon sat down at one of the tables and started a slow shuffle of a deck of greasy cards

Hatfield's eyes narrowed. He had given the man a chance to pull out, but he hadn't taken it Hatfield didn't understand about these men, but he knew that "Lanky" Reynolds was aching for a fight with Logsdon. The gun-hawk stood with his back to the bar, his elbows hooked over it, hands dropped loosely so that his fingers were not far from his gun.

"So yuh aim to hire out in these parts, Mr.—" he said to Hatfield.

"The handle is Tex Geary," Hatfield supplied. "Been down in the Big Bend the past two-three years."

"Big Bend!" Reynolds' wolf eyes glistened. "I know that country mighty good."

His lips widened in an understanding grin He winked

14

at his partner. "Then maybe yuh've crossed the Rio Grande by moonlight?"

Hatfield's drawling voice hardened.

"That's my business again, I reckon. I read my own back trail."

"No offense" Reynolds shrugged.

Logsdon had made a solitaire lay-out. He looked up, one card poised over the table.

"Another gunhawk for AX, Reynolds," he said. "Yuh can rustle more cows and blame it on the farmers. Yuh can bushwhack somebody else and blame it on us. Yuh got one more gun to force yore dirty deals down our throats."

Reynolds catapulted from the bar. Hatfield stiffened but the other gunhawk swung to face him, his six blurring out of holster and lining down.

"Logsdon has asked for trouble all along, Geary," he said softly, "and I reckon he'll get it. Yuh ain't takin' a hand, savvy?"

Hatfield's jaw hardened, but the black Colt muzzle was pointed directly at his chest and Hatfield had no doubt the man behind it would not hesitate to pull the trigger Hatfield's eyes became like green rocks, but he made no move to argue against the steady six.

Reynolds stalked to Logsdon's table and glared down at him The farmer met the angry stare, and slowly placed the deck on the table.

"Yuh talk too blamed free and loose," Reynolds said coldly "I don't like it."

"Then why did you and Ben Meacham come to the farmer's saloon?" Logsdon demanded. "AX hands use Tom Parson's place across the street."

"I go where I please."

"Yuh come here to pick a fight," Logsdon said quietly. "Yuh saw me come in and yuh follered Yuh want to gun me down or run me out of Matos like yuh have the others Well, I ain't runnin' Yuh can make yore play"

"Yuh've accused the AX of a heap," Reynolds snapped. "Yuh can eat them words or chew lead."

"Better let it ride," Hatfield spoke up.

Reynolds gave him a cold glance over his shoulder,

"Keep yore mouth shut," he snapped, and turned back to Logsdon "Talkin' turkey?"

The farmer arose.

"Shuck yore gun-belt, Reynolds. It'll be a pleasure to change yore face It'll pay back a little some of the dirty—"

Reynold's looping fist caught him squarely in the mouth. Logsdon crashed over another table and hit the floor, sprawling. For a minute he lay there, eyes glazed, mouth working Reynolds watched, his lips pulled back from his teeth in a wolfish grin.

Abruptly Logsdon rolled over and came to his hands and knees He shook his head to clear it, then came to his feet His fists doubled and he lunged forward. Reynolds stepped back and his hand slashed downward. Hatfield drew a hard breath and Meacham's six bored cruelly into his side

Reynold's six blurred upward and lined down on Logsdon In the farmer's eyes was sudden fear. He tried to claw something out of his pocket, but Reynold's Colt roared, flame lancing out Logsdon was driven backward by the slap of the slug in his chest. He fell to the floor, his legs drew up spasmodically, then abruptly went limp.

"The sidewinder tried to pull a gun on me," Reynolds said in mock injury. His wolf eyes met Hatfield's, narrowed. "I shore hope yuh saw it that way, Geary."

CHAPTER III

Bob Logsdon

Every shocked instinct in Jim Hatfield cried aloud for him to reveal his Ranger badge and arrest the two gunhawks on the spot It had been cold, deliberate murder and Logsdon had never had a chance!

But Hatfield knew that Meacham's gun and Reynold's wolfish stance meant immediate death if he protested Besides the Ranger would be exposing his own hand and the Matos case might never be solved. Reynolds and Meacham could be arrested at any time and the bartender would be a witness.

Hatfield slowly nodded. "I reckon that's the way it was," he agreed.

Reynolds' smile widened. "A smart hombre" He looked at the bartender. "What do you know about it, Baldy?"

"Just—like yuh said " The man swallowed hard.

"Put up yore six," Reynolds ordered Meacham. "Better get the sheriff Seems like he's needed here."

Meacham holstered his gun and looked down at Ray Logsdon's limp body. The bullet had caught the farmer dead center in the chest, and the man probably had been dead before he hit the floor Meacham walked to the swing doors, pushed them open, and disappeared into the night.

Hatfield turned to the bar, still fighting his impulse to blast Lanky Reynolds out of his boots In a controlled voice he ordered another drink. "Baldy" moved like a frightened automaton, his drooping eyelid twitching nervously He spilled the liquor as he poured it and Hatfield quietly pushed the glass toward him.

"Yuh need it—bad and quick "

Baldy gulped down the drink, poured another and pushed it toward Hatfield. Excited voices sounded outside and curious, frightened faces peered over the bat-wings Reynolds motioned them away.

"Been some trouble," he said. "Keep out till Kemper gets here "

The batwings opened and a paunchy man with a star on his soiled vest came in, with Meacham behind him. The sheriff's watery blue eyes swept over Hatfield, then were turned on Reynolds. He had pendulous red cheeks and his fat lips were tobacco stained. Straw-colored hair escaped from beneath his flat-crowned black hat. His soiled shirt was unbuttoned just above the heavy gun-belt that circled his paunch.

"What's wrong, Lanky?" he asked.

Reynolds gestured toward the body beneath the up-turned poker table.

"Ray Logsdon was drunk and askin' for trouble He started talking mean and pulled a gun on me. I had to sahvate him "

Kemper drew in a hard breath. "That's bad, Lanky."

"Yuh'd better look at the body," Reynolds said flatly.

Kemper turned without a word and knelt down beside Logsdon. He looked up.

"Don't see no gun, except this'n in his pocket."

Reynolds' thin lips flattened "Shore yuh didn't find it on the floor by his hand? Better make mighty shore, Sheriff."

Kemper stared blankly at Reynolds, then a look of cunning came in his watery eyes. He glanced at Hatfield and the bartender, and Reynolds laughed, a cold, deadly sound.

"Baldy won't argue none," he drawled, "and I reckon Geary here has got enough savvy to know what he saw. He's been in the Big Bend, he says, and yuh learn fast down there."

Kemper shrugged his fat shoulders and lifted a small nickel-plated revolver from Logsdon's pocket. He examined it, then stuck it in his own pocket, after dropping it on the floor beside the dead man's hand. He arose and brushed off the knees of his wrinkled trousers.

"Reckon there ain't no question it was self-defense," he

18

said evenly. "But mebbe yuh'd better head back to the AX, Lanky These nesters ain't goin' to like yuh none."

Reynolds touched his holster expressively Kemper gave Hatfield and Baldy another sharp glance, walked to the door, and pushed them open.

"Ain't no need to get excited," he said, his voice gruff and commanding. "Ray Logsdon got proddy and pulled a gun on Lanky Reynolds. Stay out till the undertaker gets the body."

"It was murder!" an angry voice shouted.

Kemper's shoulders squared "That's a lie! Reynolds has witnesses Somebody better take word out to Bob his pa's been salivated."

"Bob's in town," the same angry voice called. "Reynolds better look sharp."

Reynolds grinned at Meacham.

"I reckon we'll tally us another hoeman," he said softly.

Hatfield sensed another gun-trap being set, and this one he was determined to wreck With a show of unconcern he hitched up his holster and turned toward the batwings Reynolds' voice stopped him.

"See Deacon Matthews down the street, Geary. Tell him I sent yuh and yuh'll be on the AX payroll."

"Might do that." Hatfield nodded

Reynolds' eyes narrowed ."Yuh'd better do it. Wanderin' waddies don't find it so healthy in Matos, friend. Think it over while yuh got time."

Hatfield nodded, pushed through the crowd at the door and stepped out into the dark street. As he took a deep breath of the cool, clean air, again he had to fight the impulse to pin on his Ranger badge and make short work of the two killers in the saloon.

He stood beside Goldy, thoughtfully stroking the golden animal's soft muzzle. The men about the batwings, he thought, were like a bunch of vultures, waiting for a second killing. Bob Logsdon, Ray's son, would be looking for gunsmoke.

Hatfield rolled a cigarette, listening to the hum of excited voices He stiffened when two men hurried into the saloon. But there was no sound of gunshots from inside,

19

They reappeared in a moment carrying a limp form. Reynolds and Meacham came swaggering out, stood on the porch for a time, then strolled off down the street. Reynolds saw Hatfield and halted.

"Seen Matthews yet?" he asked.

"Not yet."

"Yuh'd better The AX pays good and yuh don't run into trouble like yuh do just wanderin' around with a loose mouth Sheriff Kemper might get plumb curious about yore past, amigo."

Reynolds walked on and the shadows swallowed him up. Hatfield remained at the hitch-rack for a while, then wandered back into the saloon Baldy sighed with relief when he saw who it was. Hatfield refused the man's gesture toward a bottle.

"Who is Lanky Reynolds?" he demanded.

"He's a hand on the AX spread," Baldy answered. "He ain't the foreman or the segundo, but he shore swings a heap of weight with Deacon Matthews, the manager."

"And he swings it with Kemper," Hatfield said dryly. "How come?"

"It ain't Reynolds that's got the swing," Baldy answered. "It's Deacon and the AX Kemper knows who elects him and who keeps him elected year after year"

"We saw murder," Hatfield said, and Baldy started sweating. "Logsdon didn't start for his gun until Reynolds' six was plumb out of leather."

Baldy swished the bar cloth and looked unhappy. His drooping lid twitched.

"Yuh're a stranger in Matos," he mumbled. "Did yuh live here, you'd not even think except what Reynolds told the lawman. Matos' Boot Hill has grown considerable the last year or so—mostly gents like you and me."

"AX?"

"Not entire. There's been killin' on both sides. Some AX hands has disappeared mighty sudden. They ain't in Boot Hill because nobody ever found 'em to bury 'em"

"A trouble range," Hatfield said. "Who was Ray Logsdon?"

"Ray was a mighty fine man," Baldy said slowly, and

glanced hurriedly toward the door. "I reckon the farmers along Matos Creek looked to him as a gent they could foller. The AX claims that creek and has brought pressure on the hoemen."

The batwings swung violently open and Baldy jumped. Hatfield whirled around. A young man stood framed there, face bloodless, his lips like a red gash above a granite chin. He wore no hat and his black hair showed that his fingers had run through it time and again. His tall body was clad in denim jacket and trousers His boots were stained with dirt, and a nickel-plated revolver was in hand.

"Where's Reynolds!" he demanded in a nerve-taut voice.

"He ain't here, Bob," Baldy said, and his fat hands made a placating gesture. "He's rode to the AX prob'ly. Yuh can't go out there "

"I'll kill him!" Bob Logsdon said wildly. "I don't care where he holes up!"

"Yuh're a locoed fool!" Hatfield snapped. Bob's eyes jerked to him and his face flushed angrily. "Put down that gun and get some sense in yore head."

Bob Logsdon's lips stretched back over his teeth.

"Cowpuncher! Gun hand! Yuh probably helped kill my father!"

"Baldy can tell yuh different. But yuh're not gunnin' for a man who's ready and waitin' for yuh."

"I'm gettin' Reynolds—tonight," the young man declared flatly "You or nobody else can stop me! It was murder, and I aim to even the tally."

Hatfield stepped away from the bar, and instantly the nickeled revolver covered him Logsdon's white face was strained and Hatfield knew he might pull trigger at the least excuse Hatfield stood straight, arms hanging loose, but his weight rested on the balls of his feet. His gray-green eyes bored into Bob's, held them.

"I don't aim to hurt yuh," Bob said, "but don't try to stop me!"

He backed toward the doors, and through them. Hatfield heard his running steps across the canopied

21

porch. Instantly he jumped to the doors and rushed through them.

Light from the stores and the saloon across the street made broad yellow beams athwart the dusty roadway and the planked sidewalks.

Hatfield glanced up and down the street but didn't see Bob Logsdon Evidently he had darted around the building and might be hurrying in any direction

Jim Hatfield swore softly. Young Logsdon would hunt out Lanky Reynolds, and a showdown could end only one way. Suddenly Hatfield recalled that Ray had accused Reynolds of deliberately entering the "farmers" saloon.

As Hatfield looked across the street, the batwings of the saloon there swung open to admit a cowboy who walked with a bowlegged roll.

Hatfield turned sharply, along the planked sidewalk. He was well beyond the saloon when he crossed the dusty street and moved silently into the shadows between the saddle shop and the cowboys' saloon.

At the far corner he halted, eyes probing the darkness. He heard voices and the clink of glassware through the flimsy walls. Light from a narrow back window disclosed a pile of rusty cans and broken bottles. Beyond, stretching into black infinity against the night sky, was the silent ocean of grass. The stars were bright, but there was no moon.

Hatfield guessed that Bob Logsdon would come to this saloon hunting Reynolds Logsdon, though killing mad, would not so completely have lost his senses as to walk in through the swing doors boldly. He wouldn't last long enough to adjust the lamplight to his eyes. He would come this way, gaining entrance through the rear.

Surprise then would give the young farmer the necessary seconds to down the man who had killed his father. In his present state of mind, the young man would not be thinking much of what happened after that.

But Ranger Jim Hatfield knew there was no chance of his coming out alive if the rest of the AX crew were like Lanky Reynolds and Ben Meacham!

Hatfield knew that he would probably have to use

22

drastic measures to save Bob' Logsdon from certain death The young man was too overwrought to think of more than avenging his father. The Ranger waited anxiously.

CHAPTER IV

Matos Mix-up

For a few tense moments Hatfield wondered if he had·
misjudged Bob Logsdon's next move There was no sign
of the young farmer, and he could easily be planning to
trap Reynolds elsewhere Hatfield rubbed his hand wor-
riedly along his jaw, then stiffened when he heard a
slight sound in the darkness.

Something moved beyond the pile of rusty cans—
moved and was silent again. Hatfield watched, silent,
tense. The movement came again, no more than the
vague flitting of a shadow, then Hatfield's keen eyes
made out the low-crouched form beside the pile of re-
fuse. Bob Logsdon's next rush would take him to the back
door of the saloon.

Abruptly Logsdon arose and came at a silent run
toward the place. Hatfield gauged the distance, then
suddenly sprang out

Bob Logsdon whirled, the nickeled revolver coming
up with the speed of light.

Hatfield struck, the full weight of his body behind his
fist. His knuckles landed high on young Logsdon's jaw
and the man sailed back, the gun flying from his fingers.
It struck the rusty cans with a metallic clang Logsdon
bounced to his feet and came charging in.

He made no sound but fought with a killing fury.
Hatfield met his rush head-on, blocked a sizzling hay-
maker, and sank his left into the young man's midriff.
Bob doubled over but instead of falling, savagely butted
his head into Hatfield's chest. Both men were carried
backward.

Logsdon clawed for one of Hatfield's holstered sixes
and had one half out of leather before the Ranger's steel
fingers settled around the young farmer's wrist. Again
Logsdon tried to use his head as a battering ram and

Hatfield sank two punishing blows into the man's ribs. Logsdon broke away

"Yuh killin' snake!" he gasped, and came charging in again.

The fight went at too fast a pace for Hatfield to do any explaining It took all his energy and breath to beat off the savage attacks.

Logsdon abandoned his fists, and sought to lock his arms around his adversary in a backbreaking bear-hug. Hatfield punched at his face and stomach but Logsdon bore in.

As yet neither man had raised his voice but Hatfield knew that sooner or later someone in the saloon would hear the fracas If Reynolds came out, he might use the fight as excuse to finish the killing job he had started on Ray Logsdon.

Bob's clutching fingers sank like talons into Hatfield's shoulders He jerked the Ranger forward, smashed lips grinning in triumph Hatfield gauged the man's jaw and let drive a pile-driver fist against it He connected squarely and solidly. Bob went down as though he had been shot

Without hesitation, Hatfield bent down and struggled to pick up the dead weight He staggered to his feet and made slow progress off into the darkness. Well beyond the radius of the lamplight, he dropped his burden and sat down beside it. His head lifted when he heard voices.

Men came out the rear door of the saloon One of them held a lantern. They walked aimlessly around between the building and the trash pile.

I tell yuh there was one whale of a fight goin' on!" one man's voice complained loudly. "I got just a glimpse of it through the window upstairs, and come runnin' to tell yuh "

"First it's pink elephants," another voice jeered, "and then it's fights. Don't see nothin' now, do yuh?"

"No, but cuss it—"

"Go sleep it off," growled a third voice which Hatfield believed to be that of Reynolds "Yuh're so spooked because of Ray Logsdon, yore imagination has done run wild Anything comes of it, I'll handle it—easy."

The men trooped back into the saloon and silence settled over the town. Hatfield sighed and bent over Bob. The young man was still out and Jim Hatfield deeply regretted the marks his fists had left on the young man's face Bob would have a lot of explaining to do. Better that, though, than dead

Logsdon groaned and Hatfield clapped his hand over the young man's mouth. Bob suddenly sat up.

"Where am I?" he demanded.

"Yuh're still alive," Hatfield answered. His six jumped out of the holster and buried its muzzle in Logsdon's stomach "Don't get any loco ideas yuh can start the fight again I'm plumb tired of beatin' sense into yore head"

"Yuh're—the AX gunhawk," Bob said, with growing anger

"If yuh'd listen instead of beller and fight," Hatfield snapped, "yuh'd know better I ain't on nobody's payroll, Logsdon Get that in yore thick skull and keep it there."

Bob Logsdon glared.

"But yuh was at the saloon when Father was gunned down!"

"So was Baldy, but he had nothin' to do with it. Shore, I carry sixes but that's no sign I ride around shootin' folks."

"Reynolds did—my pa. You or nobody else can stop me from sendin' that snake to Boot Hill"

"I don't want to," Hatfield said, "when the time is right. I been tryin' to make yuh see that Reynolds expects yuh to come gunnin' for him Yuh'd be cut down on sight. Yuh'd do yoreself and yore pa no good if they put yuh beside him in Boot Hill."

Bob was silent for a time.

"I reckon yuh're right," he said then, heavily.

"I know it," Hatfield said forcefully. "What's the trouble between you and the AX spread?"

"First," Bob said shortly; "just who are you?"

"Name's Tex Geary. I got tangled up in that deal back there and I aim to know the score"

Bob motioned toward the six, still lined on his stomach.

"Yuh can point that six-gun somewheres else. Yore fists

26

were right convincing. I'll leave Reynolds alone, for tonight."

Jim Hatfield holstered his six. Bob Logsdon sighed, stared at the lights of the distant saloon, and his eyes hardened

"The AX is owned by some gents in England," he said abruptly. "They come in here years ago and bought up a little stretch of land north of Matos along Skull Creek. They appointed a manager—a foreman, he was—to run the spread and another up in Denver to act as business and bankin' agent for them The real owners ain't seen this place over twice since they bought it."

"There's others like it" Jim Hatfield nodded "Generally syndicate spreads are run mighty peaceful and efficient"

"So would the AX be if the manager who first come here was still in the saddle But he got killed several years ago Deacon Matthews was *segundo* then and he was appointed manager He's his own foreman now, with a segundo who stays on the ranch all the time Deacon had ideas of his own about the AX and the country roundabout He began to expand AX range till they grazed thousands of acres and set up a camp along Matos Creek to handle the beefs they grazed south of the town The AX had no legal claim to any of that range and they didn't do nothin' to prove up on it."

"Open range idea," Jim Hatfield said softly.

Bob nodded "Open range. Deacon figgered that was the law, and for years there wasn't nothin' to prove him wrong But the railroads had built through here and the Government gave it a subsidy in land. Matos Creek was part of that subsidy and the railroad land office sold it for farmin' Pa and his friends bought all along Matos Creek and each one of us has a deed transferred to us from the railroad company."

Bob pulled his knees up and clasped them in his long arms He stared unseeingly at the lights of Matos.

"We hadn't heard of the AX or of Deacon Matthews," he went on "The railroad didn't mention 'em. We had bought good farmland and we spent more money on new tools, wagons to get out here, supplies to hold us till our first crops came There was blamed little dinero among any of us by the time we got to Matos Creek. We had to make a go of it or plumb starve to death."

"Then yuh learned about the AX?" Jim Hatfield suggested softly.

"Then we learned. We had started buildin' cabins when Matthews rode up. Claimed we was trespassin', that it was AX range. He got downright mean and Pa growled right back at him Matthews rode off, but come back in a day or two with the sheriff that he owns The lawman was goin' to drive us off, but when Pa showed him our deeds and surveys, Kemper couldn't do nothin', crooked as he was. Deacon Matthews was fit to be tied.

"We figgered the argument was over and we'd won, hands down." Bob's voice tightened. "We didn't savvy Deacon Matthews. The AX segundo, Tidy Hart, is a square-shooting gent. I know he planned to forget Matos Creek, figgerin' we had a claim to it But Deacon wouldn't let it go without a fight He brought in gents like Lanky Reynolds and that sidewinder, Ben Meacham. Tidy kicked like a burnt steer but had to put 'em on the payroll.

"Well, I reckon yuh can guess what happened We'd come into Matos to the stores and we'd run into gunslingers just achin' for a fight Bill Bronson and Lem Roark, two of our men, was killed. We got warnin's to leave Matos or feed the grass."

"The law?" Jim asked.

Bob laughed mockingly. "Kemper is Matthew's man. The AX elected him and the AX kept him in office If one of us so much as spit in the street, we landed in jail for a week. But a gunslinger could kill a man in broad daylight and swagger around a free man Finally Pa decided we'd better carry guns to protect ourselves All of a sudden things changed Matthews said publicly that mebbe we had a right to Matos Creek land Once more we figgered we'd won "

Logsdon became silent and Jim Hatfield patiently waited His eyes were narrowed thoughtfully as he weighed the information the young farmer had given him against what little he already knew.

"First thing we heard," Bob went on then, "an AX hand had been bushwhacked. A month later another rider was found dead A third man, one of Matthew's gunslingers, disappeared. Ain't been seen since. Name was Tripp Sheriff Kemper come to our settlement with Tidy Hart and Matthews and he blame near give all of us the third degree. Then we heard that AX beef was beginnin' to disappear Matthews and Kemper claimed the trails disappeared blame close to Matos Creek."

"Any of yore men?" Hatfield asked swiftly.

Bob sighed.

"I don't know, Geary. There's some of us that shore ain't angels, and all of us was feeling a tight pinch. Crops hadn't come in, and some of the men got discouraged and let their work slide. Pa kept 'em hanging onto their farms. Might be some of them decided rustlin' was a quick way to get money and food. None of us like the AX any, and it might be they figgered rustlin' and bushwhackin' was a slick way to strike back. Pa and me done a heap of ridin', and asked a heap of questions. We never got a lead, but the AX rustlin' kept up.

"About that time, we got a letter from the owner in England, offering to buy our farms. Brant Trimpe, their business manager, was to come down from Denver and dicker with us Geary, we'd have been glad to sell out for a reasonable offer. Mebbe Trimpe would have made it—but he never got a chance."

"Bushwhacked, too?"

"No. Pa and some of the others had one meetin' with him at Matthews' office here in town. Pa could tell Deacon was plumb against the meetin', but Trimpe was the boss Trimpe said he was investigatin' the railroad grants and our purchase. He claimed we had a title to our ground. We was to list the improvements we'd made and submit 'em, and he'd buy us out at a decent figger. Two days later we heard Trimpe shot and killed hisself while cleanin' a gun "

"Shore it was an accident?" Jim Hatfield asked sharply.

"It might have been," Bob answered. "Some of us figgered it come at a mighty nice time for Matthews I know Tidy Hart was satisfied Trimpe had been blamed careless Anyhow, things went right back where they was before More AX beef has been stole, gunhawks try to pick fights in Matos, and tonight Reynolds shore got his wish. Pa was our leader, Geary We looked to him—and now he's gone."

CHAPTER V

The Test

Hatfield arose and stretched. He stood straight as a lance against the starlight, looking toward Matos. Bob Logsdon remained seated, his shoulders rounded in discouragement.

"I'm just a chuckline rider," Hatfield said slowly, "but seems to me if I was you I'd sort of take over my pa's job. I'd make shore who was stealin' them beefs and who killed the AX riders There's a heap of things I'd want to know before I got myself salivated."

Bob looked up. "Yuh make sense, Geary. I reckon I was plumb wrong about yuh, and I apologize here and now."

"No need for that." Hatfield smiled quickly, then sobered. "I was always a curious gent, always stickin' my nose in other folks' business. Might be I'll hire on at the AX to see what I can find out for yuh."

"But I've already got—" Bob hesitated, chuckled. "Yuh see, Tidy Hart's daughter and me have been kind of courtin'. Nobody knows about it but Clarice and me. She tells me what she can about the AX plans I was with her tonight when—Pa was killed."

"Then yuh believe Tidy Hart is straight?"

"As they come," Bob said forcefully.

Hatfield hitched up his gun-belts.

"Mebbe then he don't know all that goes on at the AX. Might be that a rollin' stone like me, pretendin' to hire his guns, could learn a heap on that spread Yes, I think I'll buy a stack of chips. Never did like to see a bunch of range wolves work Reckon yuh can trust me?"

Bob Logsdon considered, and Jim Hatfield liked the young man the better for it At last Bob arose and made a wide-flung gesture with his hands.

"What else can I do? Yuh've talked and beat sense into

31

me tonight. Yuh saved my life. The way yuh wear them sixes, yuh look like another gunwolf But I got a hunch to back yuh. Things can't get no worse than they are"

"Then if I ride for the AX—" Hatfield began.

"I'll trust yuh," Bob said simply.

The two men sealed the compact by a firm handclasp. "Then head back to the farm and stay away from Matos," Hatfield ordered. "Yuh're just an invitation for a slug. Line up the farmers behind yuh. I'll get word to yuh when it's necessary."

Bob's shoulders squared, he nodded and walked off in the darkness Hatfield turned to look at the lighted cowboys' saloon, the Punchers' Rest.

"Farmers salivated and punchers murdered and disappearin'," he mused. "Beefs stolen Pressure brought on the farmers to pull stakes from Matos Creek so's AX can be king-pin Crooked law and gun renegades—yet the owners write to the Rangers for help It's a deadly brew of the devil hisself."

He adjusted his holsters with a decisive movement and walked toward the saloon

The Punchers' Rest was crowded with AX riders The bar was deep-lined with stubble-faced, gunhung men who plainly showed the marks of the long trails. Smoke hung in long blue streamers, eddying around the lamps high above the bar and tables.

Hatfield pushed through the batwings and up to the bar The man next to him gave him a sharp look, and said something to his companion. The whisper raced around the room and conversation stopped

Hatfield felt suspicious stares bore into his back as he quietly ordered He noticed that there seemed to be another type of cowboy at the tables. These seemed to be bona-fide, hard-working punchers, neither drifters nor law dodgers. Yet they were just as keen as the others in their scrutiny of Hatfield, seemingly just as suspicious.

A man pushed away from the bar, hitched up his gun-belt and walked truculently toward Hatfield. The others, grinning, made room for him Hatfield paid full attention to his drink until the man tapped him on the shoulder with a thick, grimy finger.

Hatfield turned, slowly and easily. The man's coarse face was drink-reddened. His nose had been flattened in some barroom brawl, his grin disclosed tobacco-stained teeth, and his eyes were like chips of flint.

"It ain't often we have strangers in this place," he said, "because it ain't often we allow 'em. Even then we're mighty particular."

"Meanin'?" Hatfield asked coldly.

"Meanin' mebbe we don't want you."

"I generally stay in a place till I'm tired of it," Hatfield said quietly, "and leave when I'm ready. Any objections?"

The man's answer was a swift play for his gun. Hatfield lunged forward and his fist sank into the fellow's beefy paunch He doubled the man over, then straightened him up with another blow that left his chin wide open Hatfield's third punch cracked loudly, and the man went down. Instantly Hatfield backed to the bar and his twin Colts blurred from leather, covering the crowd.

"Any more argurments?" he demanded.

They stared at him in slack-jawed amazement. The mountain of flesh on the floor lay sprawled and unmoving Hatfield noticed quiet smiles on the faces of some of the men at the tables and he began to wonder if they were on the AX payroll.

The batwings opened and instantly one of Hatfield's guns swiveled to cover them. Lanky Reynolds drew up sharp, startled surprise on his wolf face. His eyes cut to the man on the floor, circled the gunhawks at the bar and the quiet men at the table, returned to Hatfield.

"Not many men can beat Ozark to the draw and stretch him out like that," he said quietly.

"He asked for trouble," Hatfield answered "He got it."

"I can shore see that. Put up them irons. I got a friend who wants to see yuh—about a job."

Hatfield slowly dropped his guns into holsters. Men clustered around "Ozark," who was sound asleep from Hatfield's punch. The Ranger followed Reynolds out the door and then walked slowly along the planked sidewalk

"I been looking for yuh," Reynolds said. "But yuh plumb disappeared."

"I smelled gun trouble," Hatfield answered.

"Oh, Logsdon." Reynolds chuckled. "I reckon I could take care of any nester who wanted an argument. Yuh're from the Big Bend, yuh say?"

"Yes"

"Don't aim to talk much about it?"

"None whatever," Hatfield snapped, and Reynolds laughed again, sounding pleased.

"I think yuh'll do. But the Deacon'll have to decide that I might tell yuh Deacon Matthews runs this town and the county. He's manager of the AX and a mighty important hombre in these parts. Keep it in mind when he talks to yuh, and might be yuh'd better answer his questions. A heap can depend on it"

When they reached the bank building, Reynolds turned into a hallway that opened on steep steps dimly lit by a bracketed lamp at their head. The stairs were uncarpeted and their jingling spurs sounded doubly loud. At the head of the steps was a short hall and a broad beam of yellow light came through an open door.

The room into which the door opened was an office, a small, box affair, lined with shelves on which dusty law books sat in prim rows A man arose from behind a rolltop desk.

"This is the gent I told yuh about," Reynolds said "He'd just downed Ozark when I found him"

"Ozark dead!" the man said, in a raspy voice.

"Just sleepin'," Reynolds said wryly. "This gent used his fists But them guns of his come out mighty fast and he had the whole crew covered when I come in"

"Violence and strife!" the other man sighed "How much there is in the world! If we could only all settle our disputes in a peaceful, civilized manner. Won't you sit down, Mr —"

"Geary," Hatfield volunteered. "Tex Geary."

"I am John Matthews." The man held out a big bony hand that was as limp as a dish rag and about as greasily moist "Some people call me Deacon How I wish I could hold that office in some little country church, serving the

34

community to the best of my poor abilities! Sit down, Mr Geary."

"Deacon" Matthews was a tall rail of a man Sparse gray hair partly covered his high dome. His forehead was a veritable buttress of bone, the dry, yellowish skin broken by deep wrinkles The washed gray eyes sat deep in the sockets and the knife-edged long nose gave his face a horselike appearance that was accentuated by the lantern jaw His lips were thin, harsh, uncompromising, bounded by two deep lines that ran from his flared nostrils to the jawbone. His lips barely moved when he talked and he made a mistake when he smiled. It gave the macabre effect of a skull with a wide grin.

A thin string tie dangled loosely from his white collar. A long black coat and black trousers adorned his awkward, bony frame. He had a habit of steepling his knobby fingers, and his unctuous voice made Hatfield think of the professional tone of an undertaker.

His gray eyes probed Hatfield, dropped to the matched Colts, and traveled over the Ranger's broad shoulders.

"Where are you from, Mr. Geary?" he asked abruptly.

His scant brows arched when Hatfield mentioned the Big Bend He sighed and shook his head.

"That is a lawless country, Mr. Geary. I often shudder at the horrible tales that come from there" He looked at Hatfield sharply. "I—ah—assume you never met many lawmen down there?"

Hatfield glanced at Reynolds, who gave him a quick nod The Ranger grinned crookedly.

"Not many—and only when I had to. Lawmen and me —" He broke off with an eloquent shrug

"I am afraid you, too, are a man of violence," Matthews said, and there was something like a purr in his voice. He pointed a long finger toward Hatfield's holsters. "Might one call those the tools of your trade?"

"These Colts! Well, they've helped me out of considerable tights."

"Ah, gently put." Matthews leaned forward. "Would those—tools—be for hire, Mr. Geary?"

Hatfield was enjoying the game he was playing. He

looked at Reynolds and Matthews, suspiciously, fitting himself into the role of a shady wanderer from a lawless land.

"From yore talk, I figgered yuh didn't like trouble," he said.

Matthews made a sadly resigned gesture with his hands.

"I don't. But often evil men force us to use methods that we abhor. I am in just such a position, unfortunately for me, and probably to your gain. At the moment, I am in need of men with your—gifts, shall we say?"

"Such as?"

Matthews' lips pursed in irritation. But at last he came out with it.

"Gun speed for one, Mr. Geary. My spread faces a problem with peculiar angles that Mr. Reynolds can explain if you sign on. Because of those angles, I offer good pay, fine quarters, and a sanctuary, shall we say, for those who detest the sight of a law badge."

Hatfield laughed.

"Matthews, yuh lay yoreself wide open to a gent who's a total stranger. Suppose I turned yuh down and then told the sheriff or somebody what yuh offered?"

"That"—steel was in the unctuous voice—"is not likely to happen, Mr. Geary. I am a fair judge of character and so is Mr. Reynolds. We seldom make mistakes I own the sheriff, lock, stock and barrel. He does as I direct. Aside from that, I don't think you'd live long enough to talk much. I regret these harsh words, but they make things clear, I hope."

"Blasted clear," Hatfield said curtly. "In other words, I take yore offer—or else?"

"Or else." Matthews' smile returned. "You're up from the Big Bend—a long trip, Mr. Geary. Few make it unless they have urgent need to take heed of their health. Am I right?"

Hatfield pretended to surrender. His tone held just the right note of admiration.

"I reckon we don't need to play hide-and-seek no more. Yuh're too smart. What's the deal?"

Matthews leaned back and steepled his hands, triumphant as a cat that had just captured a mouse.

"You're on the AX payroll now, Mr. Geary. Your pay is a hundred a month, and your guns may be called upon to earn it. You are to keep your mouth shut, obey orders from myself or Mr. Reynolds, and say nothing. Officially you will work under Mr. Hart at the AX and take his orders. Actually, mine or Reynolds' supersede them."

"Anything else?"

"Keep with the AX crowd when you come to town and get friendly with no one else Mr. Reynolds can answer any further questions you may have. Good night, Mr. Geary. We are pleased to have you as one of us."

He swung around to the desk and abruptly busied himself with some papers.

Reynolds jerked his thumb toward the door. Hatfield picked his Stetson up from the floor and followed the gunhawk into the hall and down the stairs. When they reached the sidewalk, the Ranger looked up toward the lighted windows.

"Seems like this range has some mighty queer ducks living on it."

"And some dangerous ones," Reynolds added sharply. "If yuh want to stay healthy don't tangle with that gent back there "

CHAPTER VI

The AX Spread

Reynolds and Hatfield returned to the Punchers' Rest. Ozark had recovered consciousness and stood at the bar, mouthing curses about the fight. Turning, when Reynolds entered, he caught a glimpse of Hatfield He pushed his bulk away from the bar, eyes narrowed, chin thrust out.

"That's the jasper I aim to salivate!" he declared flatly.

"Calm yore feathers, Ozark," Reynolds snapped "Yuh ain't starting any trouble. Boys, meet Tex Geary. He's on the AX payroll."

The men at the bar nodded coldly, and Hatfield instantly noticed how the men at the tables stiffened a little, eyed him, their faces inscrutable. Again he had the impression that the men in the saloon represented two factions, somehow opposed to one another.

"Lanky," Ozark sputtered, "that gent and me has some unfinished business."

"Then yuh'll hold off it," Reynolds said. "Leastways till Geary leaves the AX payroll. It's getting late, boys. Down yore redeye and let's ride."

Ozark glared at Hatfield and turned back to the bar. Reynolds turned on his heel and walked outside Hatfield fell in with the men who pushed through the doors, but broke away from the crowd to his horse at the hitch-rack across the street. He swung into saddle, neck-reined Goldy and fell in with the gunhung men who rode down the darkened street.

Lanky Reynolds rode up ahead in the darkness. Slouched men rode on either side of Hatfield. They said nothing but he caught the swift, sharp glances they gave him from under their wide hat brims. The lights of Matos were soon behind the AX riders and once more

Jim Hatfield had the impression that he was crossing a great and silent sea.

The stars were bright jewels set in a bowl above him. The night limited his vision yet he felt that everywhere about him was limitless space with no boundary. Only the creak of leather and the soft thud of hoofs in the dusty road broke the silence of these plains.

Someone lit a cigarette and the match flamed high, outlining a coarse face. Another started a ribald song, but after a few bars it faded. Once Hatfield saw the gleam of a light far ahead. It slowly grew larger, seemed to circle to his right and then was gradually pin-pointed behind him.

"Cussed nesters!" the man next to him muttered, and spat in the general direction of the light

Reynolds led his crew at a steady pace for more than an hour. Hatfield had begun to wonder how far the AX headquarters might be when he saw a shadowy break in the straight line of the horizon. Then he saw that there were a few trees ahead, generally the sign of a stream in this Panhandle country He saw lights that gradually became larger.

Abruptly the cavalcade swung off the main trail, someone opened a gate, then the band moved through it. The trees loomed closer and now Hatfield could distinguish the dark bulk of buildings clustered beneath the cottonwoods The posts of a corral loomed close, and the band halted.

Hatfield dismounted with the rest Now that they were home, the men felt more free to talk Reynolds came through the group and gave the new hand brief directions about where to leave his saddle and bridle after Goldy had been turned loose into the corral with the other horses.

Then Reynolds led the way to a long, low bunkhouse. When a lamp was lighted Reynolds' hard eyes checked over the tiered bunks that lined each wall There were a few small square tables in the cleared space, a potbellied stove, cold now. The floor needed sweeping and the table tops a good scrubbing.

"Put yore gear over there, Geary" Reynolds motioned to the far end of the room. "That lower bunk to the right is yores."

Hatfield moved across the room. There were at least twenty men in the place and every one of them was of the shifty gunhawk type. Hatfield wondered about the others who had been in the saloon He dumped bedroll and rifle onto the bunk, sat on its edge, watching the men.

Not a one of them, he judged, but had stolen cows, or killed his man It was a strange crew for a big syndicate ranch to gather, particularly when the owners had appealed to the Texas Rangers. It simply didn't make sense. These men hated and feared the law, would instinctively do everything they could to fight it.

A shadow suddenly blotted out the lamplight and Hatfield quickly looked up. Ozark stood before him, thick legs planted wide, hamlike fists on his hips. His ugly face was twisted in a scowl.

The other men were silent, watchful. Reynolds was gone and the bunkhouse door closed.

"I don't like for an argument to hang fire," Ozark growled.

Hatfield shrugged. "Seems like that was settled back in town."

"Not in my tally," Ozark snapped. "I wasn't lookin' for fists, and yore lucky blow downed me. I say yuh can't do it again. It was a sidewindin' trick."

Hatfield realized instantly that this lawless crew was testing him. On any ranch a new man went through a certain amount of "hooraw" before he was fully accepted. The challenge of the scowling big renegade, Ozark, could not be sidestepped.

"If yuh ain't as yellow as I think yuh are," Ozark sneered, "yuh'll face up to me right now."

Hatfield pushed himself up from the bunk. He was only half erect when Ozark's fist caught him alongside the head. Hatfield was slammed back into the bunk. Ozark howled gleefully.

Hatfield's powerful legs straightened and his bootheels slammed into the renegade's broad chest. The blow had all the power of Hatfield's anger and strength behind it. Ozark went spinning back across the room, upsetting a table and thudding against the bunks with a wall-shaking crash. Hatfield came out of the bunk, a little dizzy, but ready for Ozark's next move

The man clung to the bunks, shook his bullet head and panted for air. Abruptly his pendulous lips snapped shut and he came charging toward Hatfield. There was not much room for footwork but Hatfield knew he had to avoid those crushing arms. He poised on his toes, until the man's taloned fingers were within inches.

He slid to one side, rocked Ozark with two sizzling punches that sent the man back on his heels. Ozark recovered, but abandoned his wild rushes. Bullet head low, eyes glaring, he slowly circled, his thick fingers working. Hatfield had moved out to the center of the room, was warily watching the man.

The sudden gleam in Ozark's eyes signaled his rush, and Hatfield was ready for it. The man catapulted forward and Hatfield sidestepped into one of the tables. It crashed over but had hampered Hatfield enough so that he could not avoid Ozark. The man's fingers sank into his shoulder and the mighty muscles flexed. Hatfield was jerked toward the broad chest. Ozark's knee came up in an attempt to cripple.

Hatfield twisted and took the blow on his thigh. But Ozark's arms encircled him and terrific pressure started on the small of Hatfield's back. Both men strained, one to break loose, the other to crush and maim. Hatfield worked one arm free. He placed the heel of his palm under Ozark's rocky chin, shoved hard. The man's head went back, but the powerful arms did not lessen their hold.

Abruptly Hatfield flicked his hand over, gave a quick, chopping blow with the edge of his palm across the thick throat. Ozark strangled, his arms dropped and Hatfield staggered back, fighting the tremendous ache in his ribs. Ozark coughed and retched, face turning red. He gasped for breath, standing against the far wall, glaring at his opponent.

Without warning his hand slashed down to his holster.

Hatfield saw the move and his own hands blurred. Twin Colts snaked out of leather and one of them blasted; a split second before Ozark's six spat flame Hatfield heard the whine of the slug close by his ear, and window glass crashed

Ozark fell back as the slug slammed home. His right shoulder collapsed and the smoking six fell from slack fingers. The man grabbed his shoulder and blood trickled through the stubby fingers Hatfield stood in a tense crouch, gray-green eyes circling the men, guns ready to bark again

"You saw his play!" Hatfield snapped "Anybody else wants to take his place—fists or guns—is shore welcome"

"We're satisfied," a man answered, a touch of awe in his voice "Yuh shore can bring them shootin' irons out a-sizzlin'."

Ozark sank down on a bunk, still holding his shoulder. His beefy face was pale, and his jaw was set against the shock of the wound. Then Reynolds burst into the bunkhouse, blazing with anger. Behind him, Hatfield glimpsed another man.

"What in blue blazing Tophet!" Reynolds shouted, then he saw Ozark He glared at Hatfield "Holster them sixes, Geary. I told you rannihans not to tangle"

Hatfield shrugged, holstered one six, ejecting the shells of the other. He threw away the spent cartridge, replacing it with a fresh load and snapped the loading gate. Only then did he meet Reynolds' angry glare.

"Yore boys play rough, amigo," he said, "and yuh ain't got much control, seems like."

Reynolds whirled to face Ozark.

"Did you start the fracas?"

The man who had followed Reynolds spoke up from the doorway He was small, coming about to Hatfield's shoulders, but he had a sizable paunch. His white shirt gleamed in the lamplight. His dark trousers and small boots were immaculate A white imperial adorned precise lips and hard jaw. His nose was veined and purpled as though he and John Barleycorn had far more than a nodding acquaintance.

"What does it matter, Reynolds?" he said "One of yore killers salivated another. Too bad both of 'em wasn't killed. It would have saved somebody the trouble later."

"This is my business, Tidy," Reynolds said huffily He was angry, but was not openly antagonistic to the little man in the doorway.

"And a bad business," "Tidy" Hart said. "Fire 'em both and the AX will be better off. We've had nothin' but trouble since you and these gunhawks hired out on the AX."

Close to twenty gun-hardened men glared murderously at the little man He met their glares with a hard, proud glance, deliberately pulled a cheroot from his shirt pocket, bit off the end, and lit it.

Reynolds' fist had clenched and it was only by exercising great control that he relaxed and spoke.

"I'll take care of this, Tidy," he said. "The Deacon wants these men and figgers I can ramrod 'em. Better let me, before yuh rile up somethin' yuh can't check "

"That," Tidy replied, with a puff of blue cigar smoke, "is kind of doubtful Settle this thing and report to me in ten minutes, or I'll take my own way to clean up around here "

"The Deacon—" Reynolds started.

"The Deacon be hanged!" Tidy lashed out at him contemptuously "Yuh heard what I said Get the job done!"

He strode out of the door. Reynolds took a deep breath and expelled it in a long-drawn sigh. He made a placating gesture to the scowling men and spoke again to Ozark ·

"Get that shoulder patched up, then saddle yore cayuse. Yuh're done on the AX. If yuh're around by daylight yuh'll stop lead—if Kemper don't catch yuh first for that killin' at Tascosa "

"Lanky—" Ozark started to protest through set teeth.

Reynolds slapped him across the mouth

"Yuh got yore marchin' orders Get goin' If yuh start anything, I'll gun yuh down myself if I have to trail yuh clean into Mexico Yuh got till daylight to save yore worthless hide."

Turning his back to the cowering, wounded gunhawk,

he came to a stop before Hatfield who waited, face inscrutable. Reynolds' hard stare locked with his.

"Did you start this?" he demanded.

"Better ask somebody else," Hatfield answered. "I make no excuses to stay on no job."

"Ozark asked for it," a renegade spoke up. "Geary took his taw both ways, with fists and guns."

"That's good enough for me," Reynolds said. "Yuh're a quick-trigger gent, Geary I might ask for a sample of it some day, but *I'm* the one who'll decide who'll yuh fight. Till then, stay peaceful Savvy?"

"Unless I get prodded into something," Hatfield answered

As Reynolds left the bunkhouse the men crowded around Hatfield. He took their handshakes, backslaps and admiration with the wry thought that Captain McDowell should see his law representative now.

CHAPTER VII

Tidy Hart

Ozark, patched up, stalked from the bunkhouse without a glance at Hatfield Two men carried his bedroll and rifle out into the darkness. Hatfield was in his own bunk when they returned.

"Lit a shuck right off," one of the men reported, "though he ain't feelin' happy with that hole in his shoulder"

No comment was made, as the men rolled into the bunks and the lamps were blown out Jim Hatfield stretched out wearily. A great deal had happened since he had left the train that morning. He stared upward into the darkness, his keen brain analyzing what he had learned.

The AX puzzled him Why should the spread have such a body of gunslammers on its payroll unless deliberate war was planned against the farmers along Matos Creek? Yet, in the attitude of Tidy Hart and the cowpunchers who had sat apart at the Punchers' Rest Saloon, these gunslammers seemed to be invaders, unwanted, hated, and despised

Deacon Matthews had hired them, and he worked directly under the orders of the English owners and their business manager. His acts were official Yet it seemed that these same owners who had authorized a lawlesss spread also had appealed to the greatest law organization in the state, the Texas Rangers. AX owned Kemper, the local sheriff, and he obeyed AX orders Still, this lawman had been judged incompetent and unable to enforce law by the absentee ranch owners themselves.

Another puzzler. Who had stolen AX beef, and what had happened to AX employees who had been killed or had disappeared? That pointed directly to the farmers, but Bob Logsdon had denied their guilt. Somehow, Jim

Hatfield believed the young farmer. Tonight Logsdon had been mad with grief over the death of his father, but essentially he had a level head on his shoulders.

What about Brant Trimpe? Had his death been accidental, or deliberate murder? The man had been sent to negotiate with the farmers, who were in a mood to sell and move out from the railroad lands they had bought. That was all in favor of the AX—and the farmers.

Assume the man had been murdered, who profited? Neither side That was clear.

The AX and the law declared that Trimpe had killed himself. The farmers didn't think so and Captain McDowell had been a touch suspicious. Suppose the farmers had done it? But the farmers had lost by Trimpe's death, and if they had committed murder, the AX certainly would not cover their crime by claiming the man had died accidentally.

Hatfield sighed. This case was murky with unknown motives and puzzling angles. It bristled with seemingly insurmountable obstacles Apparently the AX had moved to improve its own position at one time and then deliberately turned against its best interests at another. The same thing seemed true of the farmers.

Deacon Matthews, Bob Logsdon, Brant Trimpe, Lanky Reynolds and Tidy Hart were as yet unknown factors, and they were the keys to the problem. Jim Hatfield's eyes grew heavy and he drifted off to sleep, still vainly trying to shove the pieces of the puzzle around to make a recognizable picture. . . .

The loud clanging of the cook's triangle awakened him the next morning. Hatfield rolled out of his bunk and followed the rest of the men outside to the long racks that held wash basins Seen by daylight, the AX spread looked big and prosperous. The white house was a low, sprawling building in a grove of cottonwoods, with a veranda running along two sides. There were two bunkhouses, the one in which Hatfield had slept having been converted from some other use. Possibly it had been a long tool shed.

The corral was a big one with high, stout posts. Beyond it loomed the barn, the winter feed racks. A smithy and a cookshack that stood beside a sprawling wagon house completed the buildings. Dust already arose from the corral where a band of punchers were riding out to head for the open range Hatfield caught their cold, aloof glances and again had the distinct impression that there were two crews on the AX spread. His own group were trouble-hunters.

He ate with that group, and along the tables did not see any man he would have branded as a hard-working puncher- Every man had a touch of the wild about him. Hatfield had nearly finished when Reynolds came in.

"Tidy Hart wants to see yuh, Geary," he said "He'll give yuh strict orders to mind yore own business and keep yore sixes in leather" Reynolds chuckled and the hard men around Hatfield grinned crookedly. "Listen right good to Tidy—but do as I say. Savvy?"

Hatfield left the cookshack and approached the back door of the big house. Just as he reached it, the screen opened and a lovely girl stepped out. She stopped short when she saw Hatfield and her clear violet eyes swept over him from broad shoulders to narrow hips.

Her red lips curled with contempt as Hatfield swept off his hat.

"You're the new hand Deacon Matthews hired?" she asked in a clear voice.

"Yes, ma'am Tex Geary's the name"

"I have no interest in your name or you," she said coldly. "My father will talk to you in the kitchen"

She marched off toward the stables, Hatfield watching her.

She was a tall girl with a lithe, slender body Deep chestnut hair swept from beneath the brim of the flat-crowned hat she wore, and was held in a bun on· the back of her neck The sun of Texas had deepened her clear skin to a rich cream color, and the oval of her face was accented by her dimpled chin In buckskin riding skirt, leather jacket, and open-throat white shirt, she was the loveliest girl Hatfield had seen in a long time

"No wonder Bob Logsdon is in love," he told himself, "if that's Clarice Hart"

He knocked at the door and a petulant voice ordered

47

him to come in. When he entered the kitchen Tidy Hart sat at the far end of a big table, bathed in sunlight from the big window. He looked smaller than ever, but he had the frowning dignity of a Napoleon Though early in the morning, he was dressed as if he had just stepped from a bandbox His white hair looked like shining silver in the sunlight. He delicately touched his sweeping mustache. Only the red-bruised nose denied the general impression of brisk efficiency.

"Yuh're Tex Geary?" he demanded.

He poured a touch of whisky into his steaming coffee, stirred it. Not once did his hard, probing study of Hatfield waver He sipped the brew and smacked his lips, but made no motion to offer Hatfield a chair or a drink.

"That's me," Hatfield drawled.

"Deacon Matthews hired yuh in Matos," Tidy stated flatly. "Why?"

"Well"—Hatfield carefully felt his way—"because I'm a good hand, I reckon I've had the right experience."

"Ah!" Tidy's brows arched high. "The right experience, eh? Knowin' how to use a Colt, or pick a fight?"

Hatfield shifted his weight, his fingers tightening on his hat brim He did not reply, and Tidy Hart sipped his spiked coffee The AX segundo's eyes lost their fire and his voice became more pleasant.

"I sized yuh up as a different sort of hombre, Geary, and I'm generally a good judge of men. I don't know anything about yore past—don't want to know. But the AX will give yuh a chance to make somethin' of yoreself if yuh foller orders"

Hatfield still remained silent, his gray-green eyes shrewdly watching the little segundo A look of annoyance flitted over Tidy's face, and his voice became brisk again

"That's up to you, Geary, but here are yore general orders. Keep yore six in leather. It's not to be used against any man Leave the farmers' alone We're havin' a little trouble with 'em, but the owners and managers can handle that legally You do yore range work and leave the rest to us. Savvy?"

48

"I savvy," Hatfield answered briefly.

Tidy gave him a sharp look, grunted, and sipped his coffee again.

"Matthews is hirin' the kind of men I wouldn't allow on the AX," he said. "I can't help that, but I'm segundo here by order of the owners. That's something even Matthews can't change I expect my orders to be obeyed. That'll be all, Geary, for now."

Jim Hatfield nodded, and walked out of the house, spurs jingling Outside, as he shoved his hat on his head, he caught a glimpse of Clarice riding off across the range Reynolds stood by the yard gate, waiting for him, a crooked grin on his lips. Meacham stood a few feet away, whittling on a stick.

"Yuh got yore orders?" Reynolds asked when Hatfield came up. He laughed at the new man's answer. "Tidy makes a loud beller, but that's all. Yuh noticed he didn't assign yuh to any crew or any particular work He knows better. Matthews wants us boys for special jobs."

"Mighty funny setup," Hatfield said briefly.

"That's none of yore worry, Geary Tidy pretends he's king-pin, and we let him think it We do just enough range work that he can't complain to the owners. But Tidy knows where he stands, though he won't admit it. Yuh'll ride line with Ben Meacham here today so yuh'd better saddle up."

Hatfield whistled to Goldy and the horse came trotting to the corral gate He saddled up while Meacham admiringly watched the sprinted, golden horse.

The two men rode out across the great ocean of grass. And again Hatfield felt the power of this great sweep of country.

"Over yonder," Meacham interrupted his thoughts, "is the farmers along the lower stretch of Matos."

Hatfield's eyes followed the direction of Meacham's pointing finger A line of trees marked another creek. Little white squares gleamed in the bright morning sun— distant farm houses, and south of them were the cultivated fields of the nesters.

"Lanky always sends a new man line-ridin'," Meacham

49

observed "It's the quickest way to learn the spread. If there's any night ridin', yuh'll know yore way around."

"Much of that?" Hatfield asked lazily.

"Just now and then. Lanky'll tell yuh all yuh need to know when the time comes."

Meacham changed the subject, began a rambling tale about a card game in Matos that had ended in a gun fight Hatfield only half-listened He was beginning to understand Tidy Hart's position Probably Tidy once *had* been king-pin on the ranch with the manager handling only the buying and selling of beef, and other financial matters for the syndicate.

But Matthews had made a change, and Tidy had found himself superseded He had been helpless to stem an influx of hardcases on the payroll, and his authority had been undermined by Matthews' instructions to such men as Reynolds Tidy was not a man who would acknowledge defeat, so he still clung to the pretense of ruling the AX.

Hatfield shrewdly judged the little bantam He talked big, stubbornly made his claims But Tidy was secretly worried and more than a little frightened by the gunhawks who followed Lanky Reynolds Tidy was not personally afraid of any one of them, but the little segundo realized that this bunch of dangerous killers were beyond his control in case of a showdown Hatfield wondered if that could be the reason for Tidy's drinking.

Just ahead a fence showed high and black against the blue horizon and Meacham rode directly toward a wide gate. On the other side, the renegade forgot the card game story. He jerked his thumb back toward the fence.

"That marks the boundary of land that the AX filed on," he explained. "We claim the rest of this for miles in every direction, but seems like there's some argument about it. Heard Reynolds say title would be completed on some more land in a week" He chuckled "If it is, them farmers will be plumb surrounded."

CHAPTER VIII

Range Killing

The trip around the claimed boundaries of the AX took three days There were some fences, but these had been erected by neighboring spreads and few of them joined.

Ranger Jim Hatfield saw several herds of cattle, sleek and fat creatures bearing the AX brand. Twice he and Meacham met AX punchers, the real workers on the ranch Invariably these men were cold and distant, anxious to avoid the gunslingers who had invaded the AX.

Hatfield had a clear picture of the ranch by the time they rode toward its sprawling buildings again Evidently Matthews and the new business manager clung to the open range theory, refusing to fence, making wide grazing claims to lands that were open to homesteading. The advent of the farmers in the very heart of the range had awakened the owners, and they were taking steps to acquire title. Title assured, they were reluctantly fencing.

It was late afternoon when Meacham and Hatfield dismounted Meacham unsaddled, and turned his horse into the corral, clumping away to the bunkhouse. But Hatfield saw that Goldy was watered and fed, then worked on the golden coat with currycomb and brush.

An hour passed before Hatfield finished He had started toward the bunkhouse when he caught sight of a rider coming at a fast lope. And even at the distance Hatfield's keen eyes saw that a limp form lay across a second horse Hatfield's eyes narrowed.

The ranchhouse door slammed and Tidy Hart came running out into the yard.

"Who's that?"

"Looks like Reynolds," Hatfield answered. "He's bringin' somebody in."

᛫ "Gunslammer killin' again!" Tidy cursed, and glared at the men who piled out from the bunkhouse.

Reynolds rode into the ranch yard Hatfield needed only a glance to know that the man on the led horse was dead Reynolds drew rein and looked down at Tidy.

"It's Stumpy Calvert," he said. "A rifle slug got him." He seemed to be narrowly observing the effects of the killing on the little segundo.

"Who?" Tidy asked.

"Don't know," Reynolds answered, "but I can do a heap of guessin'. Where'd yuh put Stumpy to work?"

"On—Matos Creek," Tidy said, with unhappy hesitation.

"Nesters ain't far from there, and they claim that whole district. Who else'd get mad if an AX hand worked in that direction?"

"Might be that," Tidy slowly admitted. "But it could have been anybody else."

"Just who?" Reynolds demanded, with elaborate sarcasm

His face tightened angrily, and he swung out of saddle. As he cut the dead man loose Hatfield saw that the slug had caught the man squarely between the shoulder blades He had been drygulched, killed without warning.

"I'm ridin' to Matos," Reynolds snapped. "Matthews and Kemper should know about this pronto. There's times I think the AX has a heap too much love for nesters."

"That'll be enough, Reynolds," Tidy snapped "I'm still segundo here. Ride to Matos and get the sheriff. We'll have a posse waitin' when he gets here "

Reynolds grinned crookedly and led his horse to the corral while the punchers took the limp body toward the ˉbuggy shed Reynolds roped another horse, changed saddles, and streaked toward distant Matos.

Hatfield caught a glimpse of Clarice on the porch, saw the excited way she turned into the kitchen with her father as Tidy hurried back to the house.

Hatfield went to the bunkhouse. Three men were playing cards at one of the rickety tables They gave Hatfield brief nods as he strode to his bunk. He pulled up short. Someone had been through his roll.

"What gent got nosy?" he demanded harshly.

One of the card players looked up, feigning surprise.

"What yuh talkin' about, Geary?"

"Somebody has gone through my bedroll. Who was it?"

"Shucks! I don't know! I ain't seen no one around yore bunk, Geary How about you boys?"

The other two shook their heads. Hatfield knew they were lying.

"All right," he said quietly, "yuh don't know. But the next time this happens, I figger on gunsmoke Yuh can pass the word around."

He stretched out on his bunk and the three men went on with their card game. Jim Hatfield knew that someone had tried to check on his story about the Big Bend, but they had found nothing.

His silver star was snugged in a secret pocket, safe enough from prying fingers and curious eyes Reynolds had undoubtedly sought some further line on the new hand's past.

Tidy Hart popped in the doorway.

"Yuh can get ready to ride with the sheriff when he comes," he said shortly. "The AX will form the posse."

The segundo disappeared and the three men stared at the door, surprised.

"Stumpy Calvert," one of them said thoughtfully. "He was one of the old hands here. Tidy liked him a heap. Well, reckon mebbe we'd better oil our sixes."

Reynolds came back several hours later, and with him was Sheriff Bill Kemper and Deacon Matthews. The three of them disappeared into the ranchhouse, and when they came out, after some time, Tidy frowned at their swaggering backs from the porch.

"Hit yore saddles—pronto!" Reynolds' bull bellow sounded over the yard. "We got us some manhuntin' to do!"

Hatfield mounted Goldy while the rest milled around Matthews and Kemper. Only the gunhawks were called for the posse, Hatfield instantly noticed, and his lips thinned grimly. It looked as though trouble were expected, maybe hoped for. Tidy still stood on the porch, but Clarice was not around. Hatfield hadn't seen her since "Stumpy" Calvert had been brought into the yard.

At last all the men were mounted. Reynolds swung into leather, and, at a brief nod from Kemper, led the way out of the yard.

With the hardcase crew streaming out behind him, and Kemper and Matthews to either side of him, Reynolds headed out across the plain, and the whole cavalcade hit a fast, ground-eating pace.

Before long Hatfield caught sight of the thick bushes and trees along Matos Creek. He saw the tender new grain that the farmers had planted, and realized that Bob Logsdon's people had cultivated many acres. The crop looked promising.

At a wire fence the posse slowed its pace. Reynolds drew rein and pointed to the ground.

"I found Stumpy layin' right here. I was ridin' north and heard the shot. It sounded like a rifle, so I rode down this way."

"Yuh found Stumpy," Kemper said heavily. "Saw nothin' else?"

Reynolds pointed to a clump of bushes beyond the fence on the far side of the field.

"Caught a glimpse of a gent over there Wore denims, far as I could see. Just caught the one glimpse."

"Yuh reckon he done it?" Kemper asked.

Reynolds shrugged. "Who else? Naturally, I didn't climb the fence and head for them bushes I'd of made too good a target. Didn't get another look at the hombre, like I said, but I'll bet my last peso yuh'll get a lead on him if yuh search the nester village."

Kemper looked swiftly toward Deacon Matthews.

"We'll look around here to make shore, then I'll question them farmers."

"A wise decision, Sheriff," Matthews said unctuously. "Violence is always to be dreaded and avoided, but I suppose we must meet gunfire with gunfire."

Kemper dismounted and examined the ground. There

were bloodstains on the grass where Stumpy had fallen. Hatfield sat with the rest of the men, waiting He dared not show too much interest in Kemper's movements. But he studied the bushes and judged the distance to where Stumpy had been found. A good marksman might have placed the slug between the shoulder-blades at that distance. But it would be excellent shooting. Besides, Hatfield doubted that an ambusher hiding over there could be spotted from this side of the fence. The bushes were too thick.

At last Kemper straightened and returned to his horse. He led the way along the fence and there was tension in the riders. They were entering enemy territory and knew it Hatfield saw several men loosening the sixes in the low-tied holsters.

The horsemen struck a rutted path that led from the fields and turned up it, heading toward the screen of bushes and cottonwoods. The road became wider, more used It plunged through the screen and headed toward the creek.

The farmer's village was a scattered collection of huts along one side of the stream The houses were boxlike affairs but the barns were more staunchly built. There was a single small store with a high false-front. A space between the houses served as a street.

As the posse bore down on the village, men appeared in the doorways. They darted back inside and reappeared with rifles, shotguns, and even a pitchfork or two Kemper held up his hand and the posse halted.

"I'll do the talkin'," he said swiftly "Make no move unless I give the signal. If I make an arrest, look out for trouble!"

"Might be we'd sort of crave a little trouble," Reynolds growled

CHAPTER IX

A Girl's Trust

Kemper rode out a few paces ahead of the posse and they trailed into one end of the street.

The farmers had bunched, and there were pitifully few of them. Hatfield caught brief glimpses of frightened women and children who peered cautiously from the windows and doors. Young Bob Logsdon stepped out from the band.

"Better not come any further, AX," he warned coldly. "We don't like yore kind of company."

Kemper pulled up and stared down at Logsdon, then swept the line of farmers behind him.

"There's been a killin'," he stated. "AX puncher name of Stumpy Calvert." ·

"That's none of our affair," Bob snapped.

"Might be it is," Kemper replied. "Stumpy was killed right at yore line fence. Rifle bullet in the back. A man was seen in the bushes back there."

"That's a lie!" Bob said coldly.

Reynolds cursed, but Kemper's quick gesture stopped him. The sheriff leaned forward, hands folded on the saddle-horn.

"Yuh know that every one of yore friends has been right here in yore sight all the time?" he demanded.

Bob hesitated, then slowly shook his head.

"No, I can't say that. But I know my neighbors wouldn't shoot a man down like that."

"The law calls that hearsay," Kemper said with a crooked grin, "and it ain't worth a frazzled rope in court. Considerin' what was seen, and what yuh say about yore friends, then yuh won't object to some questionin'?"

Logsdon glanced at Reynolds, Matthews and the AX gunhands behind them. Hatfield gave the boy credit when Bob spotted him in the group. His expression did not change; only the muscles in his lean jaws bunched, then relaxed.

"If it's legal, no objections. But yuh don't mind if my neighbors keep close to their guns, Sheriff—just in case things get out of hand?"

"None," Kemper grunted. "But don't start nothin' yuh might regret. Now, which of yuh was over toward the AX line early this mornin'?"

"Most of us were," Bob answered. "We worked our fields there."

Kemper looked over the group.

"Which of yuh had an argument with Stumpy Calvert?" the Sheriff asked.

No one answered. Reynolds pushed forward and gave a quick signal behind his back for his men to follow. The farmers gripped their rifles tighter. Reynolds drew rein beside Kemper.

"It ain't likely a killer'll put his own neck in a noose," he said harshly "Questionin' wastes time. I can name yore killer right now—the man I saw runnin' away from the killin' this mornin'."

"Name him," Kemper snapped.

"Bob Logsdon," Reynolds said, and his hands flashed down to his holstered Colt.

Before anyone could move, Reynolds' six centered on Bob Logsdon's broad chest. The farmers surged forward but the gunhawks had followed Reynolds' play. A dozen cocked six-guns covered the men. A tense silence held the throng.

"That's a blasted lie, Lanky Reynolds," Bob said quietly.

Reynolds grinned, but his eyes glittered malevolently.

"I've shot a man for callin' me less, Logsdon But I reckon the law can handle yuh." He spoke to Kemper, without taking his eyes from the young farmer. "This is yore man, Sheriff. I'm here and now makin' a positive identification."

"That's all you need, Kemper, according to law," Matthews' oily voice lifted to say. "It's evidence enough to hold any man. I think you should make your arrest."

"Jump through the hoop like a nice trained dog," Bob said.

"Keep yore blasted trap shut, Logsdon," Kemper said, as he flushed angrily. "Yuh got enough trouble lookin' yuh in the face without stirrin' up more. I hearby arrest yuh on suspicion of the murder of Stumpy Calvert. Comin' peaceful?"

"Yuh wish I wouldn't," Bob answered. He opened his fingers and his rifle fell to the dust. "It'd give these killers the excuse to wipe us off of AX range I'll come peaceful, but yuh won't make the charge stick. Keep that in mind, Lanky."

"I ain't worried," Reynolds said coldly.

"Yuh might be. My pa's score ain't evened yet."

Bob advanced to the lawman, arms held high above his head Kemper snapped the steel bracelets around his wrists, and Bob turned to his friends.

"No trouble," he warned. "Yuh'll only hurt yourselves. I'll be back before long and I reckon it'll be time to call a tally on the AX and its killers. Let's go, Sheriff."

While renegade guns held the farmers at bay, Bob Logsdon was roughly lifted up behind one of the gunhawks Kemper, Reynolds and Matthews closed in around the rider and captive, wheeled, and rode off. Hatfield, Colts steady in his hands, helped the AX gunhawks hold the angry farmers at bay. Had they made any attempt to rescue Bob Logsdon, Jim Hatfield would have come over to their side, and his hand would have been exposed.

Luckily, the farmers only glared and muttered, not daring to buck the steady gun muzzles The renegades backed slowly off, wheeled, and raced to join Sheriff Kemper and the rest. The farmers gathered in an angry knot, gesticulating and arguing.

When the AX riders neared the home ranch, Reynolds named Hatfield and one or two other hands to go on to Matos with Kemper and his prisoner. After a brief, low conference with Matthews, Reynolds and the rest headed for the ranch.

Logsdon rode stone-faced. He met Hatfield's eyes with the same harsh glare as he did the others, and the Ranger could read nothing in the young man's inscrutable face. Hatfield felt increased confidence in Bob. He could play a part well. He had promised to trust Hatfield, and even when the Ranger was among those who escorted him to jail, he played the game.

It was dark by the time the posse reached Matos. They rode grimly and silently to the stout jail and Bob Logsdon was led inside. Matthews, with a brief word to the men to wait, entered the jail with the lawman and his prisoner When the ranch manager reappeared he was smiling triumphantly.

"Good work, men," he said. "Go to the Punchers' Rest and tell them the drinks are all on me Be back at the ranch by midnight. Geary, I'd like to see you a minute"

Hatfield dismounted while the rest rode toward the saloon Matthews rocked back and forth, from heels to toes, greatly pleased with himself.

"Geary," he said, "Reynolds tells me that you'll make a good hand. Too bad about that little mix-up with Ozark but, in a way, I'm glad that it happened. It proved you're the type of man we want."

"Thanks," Hatfield said quietly.

"Tidy Hart has made his usual palaver, I hear," Matthews continued, and laughed. "Please listen carefully to what Mr. Hart has to say. But obey Mr. Reynolds. Things will work nicely that way. That is all, Geary. Thought you'd like to know where you stand."

"I do." Hatfield nodded. He jerked his thumb toward the jail. "What happens to the farmer?"

"I'm afraid, what with one thing and another, Bob Logsdon isn't long for this world." Matthews sighed in mock concern. "If he should happen to escape the hang-noose on a murder charge, he will undoubtedly die suddenly afterwards. Good night, Geary."

"Night," Hatfield answered and turned back to Goldy. He swung into saddle and headed up the street.

There was no work on the ranch the next day. Stumpy Calvert was buried in the little, grass-grown cemetery just outside Matos. Deacon Matthews had arranged for the preacher. Just before the body was lowered into the earth, Matthews gave a little oration. He praised Stumpy for his loyalty to the AX, deplored his demise, and promised full legal vengeance.

Hatfield listened, hat in hand, lowered eyes moving sharply to study those around him. Clarice and Tidy were deeply depressed. So were some of the men. But Reynolds and the gunslammers showed their impatience almost openly.

Again Hatfield became strongly aware that any violence on the part of the AX could be definitely ascribed to Reynolds, with Deacon Matthews backing him. That accounted for Ray Logsdon's death and Bob's arrest. But what about Trimpe? And who could have profited from the deaths of Stumpy Calvert and other AX hands? Not Matthews, nor anyone else connected with the AX.

The men returned to the AX to loaf around the bunkhouse and yard. Hatfield saddled Goldy and rode out on the range, glad to be free for a time of the lawless conversation of the gunhawks. They were treacherous snakes and their talk revealed it. In the invigorating air Hatfield inhaled deeply, to clear his lungs of the bunkhouse smell.

He rode aimlessly and Goldy appreciated the chance to exercise. Ears pricked forward, the mount tossed his head so that Hatfield had to hold a tight check-rein.

As the sun dropped toward the horizon, he headed back toward the spread, but drew rein when he saw another rider heading toward him.

It was Clarice Hart. When she pulled up, Hatfield was again struck by her beauty.

"I've been wanting to talk to you," she said at once. "Bob Logsdon told me what you did the night his father was killed."

Hatfield smiled.

"Anyone would have done the same, ma'am."

"Not anyone." She shook her head and pointed toward the distant ranch. "There's many a man on that spread who would have enjoyed another killing—particularly Bob's. He told me he trusted you, and that I was to do the same."

"I hope yuh do."

"I'm following Bob's lead," she said shortly "Ordinarily, any of Reynold's friends are lying skunks. They've invaded the AX despite all my father can do. He has written to the owners, but evidently they consider Deacon Matthews' actions as aboveboard."

"Why is Reynolds at the AX?" Hatfield asked sharply. "Why does AX hire all those gun hands?"

She shrugged.

"I don't know. Matthews started hiring them. Dad won't admit it, but Reynolds is the real segundo on the spread. The old hands support Dad but if it came to a showdown, Reynolds gunhawks would win."

"Who do you think killed Stumpy Calvert?"

"I know Bob didn't Maybe Stumpy run into rustlers and was shot Bob has sometimes wondered if some of his friends might not be lifting beefs from the AX. Deacon Matthews is sure they are. That's why he brought in Reynolds and his crew. But whoever killed Stumpy, took one more loyal man from Dad."

"I reckon we'll get to the truth of the matter," Hatfield said.

Clarice nodded, but her eyes clouded.

"We must—in time to save Bob Matthews will do all he can to get Bob out of the way so that the farmers will have no leader. I'm sure that's why Ray Logsdon was killed." Clarice leaned forward. "But I still don't understand why you're taking a hand"

"Like I told Bob," Hatfield answered easily, "I like a fair deal. I saw Ray killed and Bob arrested Seems like somebody ought to sort of set things straight. Mebbe I can do it."

"I hope someone can!" Clarice said with a sigh "If Trimpe hadn't been killed, this whole mess would be settled by now."

"He was killed accidental?" Hatfield asked.

"Yes In the bunkhouse." She glanced toward the spread. "I'd better go now. It's best for both of us if we're not seen together."

She turned toward the ranch, touching the horse lightly with her spurs.

Hatfield felt much better after the talk with her. He had at least two people on the ranch he could trust in a tight.

CHAPTER X

Rustlers!

Next morning, early, Lanky Reynolds took practically all his gunhawks out toward Matos Creek They were to check the cattle on this section of the range to determine if there had been any stealing.

Reynolds apparently didn't take his orders from Tidy Hart too seriously. He gave the area around Matos Creek and the farmers' fields only a brief survey, then headed northeast. Reaching the high wire fence of a neighboring ranch, Reynolds pulled rein. The men drew up around him. Reynolds looked searchingly in the direction of the home ranch, seemed satisfied that no one watched. He slouched easily in the saddle.

"I reckon it's time we had a little exercise, boys. Geary, we'll leave you posted here. If anybody comes from AX, head 'em over west of here. Say we found the fence cut and are checking for strays."

Reynolds grinned as Hatfield looked puzzled, staring at the stout fence. The gunman leader urged his horse to the fence, pulled wire cutters from his pocket and deliberately snapped the wires between two posts. He rubbed the fresh cut ends in the dirt.

"Naturally," he said, when he came back to the men, "when AX finds a hole in the fence it acts plumb honest. That's yore job, Geary, to keep our neighbors' cows safe on their own range and AX critters over here. Me'n the boys'll be back when we're finished"

He waved negligently to Hatfield, signaled the men and rode off at a fast pace. Hatfield dismounted and threw the reins over Goldy's head, prepared to guard the break for several hours. He didn't understand Reynolds' motives in cutting the fence, except that it covered some plan the gunhawk had in mind.

Hours passed and no one came near the fence. Goldy

grazed contentedly, and Hatfield who long since had made himself comfortable, dozed against a fence post, his hat brim pulled low to protect his eyes from the sun.

It was late in the afternoon when Goldy suddenly whinnied. Hatfield came swiftly to his feet as Reynolds and his men returned. Their horses looked as if they had been ridden fast and hard. The men's faces were dust-caked. Reynolds looked pleased, and he ordered the fence to be temporarily repaired. He grinned at Hatfield.

"I'll do the talkin' when we get home," he said. "You back me up, Geary. Yuh made yoreself a little dinero to-day, though yuh might not know it."

The sun was still an hour or so high when they rode into the AX yard. Tidy Hart came out of the ranchhouse and Reynolds assumed an angry and puzzled look.

"Some jaspers cut the fence between us and the Ramblin' M," he reported. "Me'n the boys took a long pasear but didn't see no beefs. Don't know if we lost or not."

"Ramblin' M?" Tidy exclaimed, and looked worried. "They wouldn't rustle anything."

"But somebody else might of sent cow critters through the break," Reynolds suggested.

Tidy looked blankly from Reynolds to the rest of the men. One of them suddenly stood up in the stirrups and pointed a long arm to the northeast.

"Here comes more trouble!"

Two riders were streaking toward the ranch and there was an urgency in the way they fanned their horses with their hats. They rushed into the yard and pulled up in a cloud of dust.

"Rustlers!" one of them yelled. "Thirty head or more gone!"

Tidy swore and stared wide-eyed up into Reynolds' face. He swallowed, then his face became suffused with anger. His fists clenched.

"Yuh can change hosses, Reynolds," he barked. "Send Geary for the sheriff. We're trailin' them rustlers and gettin' them cows back!"

"Start ridin'!" Reynolds roared at Hatfield, and Tidy Hart could not see the malicious light in his eyes.

The men scattered for the corral and bunkhouse and Tidy's roaring orders echoed out over the plain as Hatfield neck-reined Goldy and raced off for Matos.

He knew now where Reynolds and the men had spent the day. He knew why Reynolds had been so pleased and why he had said Hatfield had made himself some dinero. For now the Texas Ranger saw that the gunhawk, employed by the AX with a renegade crew to do his bidding, took every advantage of his position.

But Hatfield could not yet be certain about Deacon Matthews. He did not like the man. Matthews was too oily, talked too much about how he abhorred violence and gunsmoke Matthews might think the methods of the ranch owners too slow, too lenient. With a gun crew he could drive the farmers off Matos Creek and AX range in double quick order.

That, Hatfield felt certain, was Reynolds' job. But it looked as though Reynolds added to his wages by rustling his employer's cattle. Hatfield thought of the silver star in its secret pocket, and grinned crookedly. Lanky Reynolds was due for some unhappy moments as soon as the Ranger felt the time had come to reveal himself.

Kemper followed Hatfield back to the AX. They changed horses and rode on to the northeast It was night and Kemper kept checking their course by the stars At last they saw a wink of a campfire and cautiously approached it. Coming closer, they saw Reynolds, Tidy, and the crew.

Tidy Hart gave the lawman a gruff, dispirited greeting.

"The trail's plumb disappeared, Kemper Headed toward Matos Creek, and then wiped out." His eyes sparked angrily. "By Godfrey, this lawlessness must stop! If you can't control it, mebbe the Rangers can!"

"I'll do what I can," Kemper replied stiffly. He turned to Lanky. "What's yore ideas?"

"Nesters," Reynolds said readily. "We found the Ramblin' M fence cut I figger the beefs was run across Ramblin' M range toward the Palo Duro Some of the new spreads down there ain't particular what cattle gets 'em started."

"And the nesters sell cheap " Kemper nodded

Hatfield dismounted, eyes hard He hunkered down before the fire and kept his eyes toward the ground to hide his thoughts Either Kemper was a fool or he took Reynolds' suggestions as orders Twice now the lawman had acted because of Reynolds' unsupported word. . . .

In the morning when Sheriff Kemper rode out with the crew to investigate the rustling, he followed Reynolds' lead in everything almost without question He examined the cut fence and stared off across Rambling M range.

"They run the cows this way," he said flatly "I'll ride down to Matos Creek and check on them nesters "

"We can side yuh," Reynolds suggested, but Kemper looked uncertain and a little frightened.

"No need, Lanky Besides, they'll be mighty touchy about Logsdon, but they won't dare raise a ruckus with the law "

Kemper told the men to go back to the ranch Since the trail of the rustled beef had played out there was nothing the crew could do now If Kemper uncovered anything, he could call for help in making arrests

Hatfield returned to the AX with the rest The whole situation aroused his disgust and anger, but he didn't dare display his hand To the Texas Rangers no case was closed until the culprits had been brought to justice. Hatfield could break up the AX gun crew, but there had been murders done before he had come to the AX, and a murder since. Those killers were still free and their trail covered.

Nor was Hatfield sure who was backing the killing and the rustling Facts pointed to Deacon Matthews, except that the manager would not be likely to rustle beef from his own spread But suppose Deacon Matthews had hired these sidewinders on order of the absentee owners? If things got too hot, they could throw Reynolds and Matthews to the law, claiming their own innocence. Things had come close to that right now, so far as Hatfield could see. The letter appealing to the Rangers might be just such a move by the owners to protect themselves *from* justice.

Hatfield's lips thinned angrily at the thought as he rode that night toward Matos with three or four other hands who were looking forward to a spree. For the more Hatfield considered the case, the more certain he became that Deacon Matthews was the key. If Matthews was behind the killing then he should pay for his crimes. If he was merely the catspaw of more powerful men, then their identity should be established and they should be brought to justice.

Hatfield dismounted with the men before the Punchers' Rest and went to the bar with them. He nursed a single drink along while the others downed several in quick succession. When the chance came, Hatfield quietly slipped away, unnoticed.

He stood on the saloon veranda, looking down the street toward the bank. A light gleamed in Matthews' office, so there would be no chance of investigation there at the moment. Maybe later, when Matthews had gone home, Hatfield might find something of interest in the man's files.

The Ranger's eyes shifted to the jail and saw that Kemper's office was dark. Bob Logsdon would be in his cell, and there were some things Hatfield wanted to know from the young farmer.

The Ranger stepped down to the plank sidewalk and moved aimlessly along, away from the jail. Several yards away, he halted and leaned aimlessly against the wall of the darkened feed store.

No one was near to pay any attention to him. Hatfield slipped around the corner of the building and moved in silently in the dark shadows. Light streamed out from the Punchers' Rest but Hatfield could easily avoid it. He moved like a cat to within a few yards of the low black bulk of the jail. He paused there, listening, eyes straining into the darkness.

Moving along the wall to a small barred window he heard the regular breathing of a sleeping man. That would be Bob Logsdon.

"Bob! Bob!" Hatfield's whisper was low. He scanned the shadows and called again: "Bob, it's Geary."

A shadowy form appeared beyond the bars and Hatfield looked at Logsdon's wry grin.

"Thought mebbe yuh'd show up, Geary," the young farmer chuckled. "Kemper went home an hour ago, so we can talk"

"Good," Hatfield whispered. "I figured yuh'd like to know AX has lost more beefs. Reynolds blames it on yore friends and the sheriff ain't arguin' none"

"What's AX intend to do?" Bob's whispering voice tightened with worry.

"I don't know—yet Sit tight, I reckon"

"It ain't like Reynolds to do that," Bob said thoughtfully "I'd expect him to ride to Matos Creek with his gun-crew and try to blast us out of there. That's the way he likes to play."

Hatfield shook his head "Even Kemper couldn't keep Reynolds from a trial if somebody was killed on the raid, and a heap of other damage done Main thing is that somebody got them cows. Any idea who the jasper might be?"

"No more that what I've always thought," Bob sighed.

"Reynolds" Hatfield nodded. "Any idea where they could run 'em?"

"Anywhere towards Palo Duro," Bob answered readily. "They could swing a little bunch of beefs north and west there toward the New Mexico buyers. It wouldn't be much of a trick I—"

He broke off short as Hatfield whirled, hands dropping to his Colts Something had moved in the shadows of a low cottonwood Hatfield edged slowly away from the window Had one of the renegades trailed him?

Jaw hard, he slipped into darker shadows and waited.

CHAPTER XI

Release

A figure disengaged itself from the cottonwood and moved silently toward the jail, headed straight for the jail window Hatfield slid the Colts out of leather If Bob Logsdon were dead, some people around Matos would feel better. He stepped out of shadows and his gun barrel dug deep into the unknown's side.

"Lift 'em and keep quiet!" he commanded

He heard a frightened gasp. And suddenly realized that his guns menaced a tall girl in riding skirt and broad-brimmed hat.

"Miss Hart!" he said, low-voiced

"Clarice!" Bob whispered urgently from beyond the bars.

The girl laughed a little shakily.

"Geary, you made me ten years older then. I slipped up to talk to Bob."

"Then I reckon this is no place for me," Hatfield said. "I'll stand under the cottonwood and give yuh warnin' if need be."

"No—wait," she said. She turned to Logsdon. "I'm going to put the argument up to Geary, Bob. I think I'm right."

"I won't have yuh in trouble because of me," Bob said swiftly.

"You let me judge who's to get in trouble," she said confidently, and spoke to Hatfield "I know Bob didn't kill Stumpy Calvert Bob and I were together about a mile from where Stumpy was killed. We heard the shot."

"Why didn't yuh say so?" Jim Hatfield asked gravely.

Clarice made a deprecating gesture.

"Bob thought it would get me in trouble. We heard the shot and that was all. I rode home and was there when Reynolds came in with Stumpy. Naturally, I slipped away again as soon as I could and warned Bob He made me promise not to tell that he and I had been together I was hiding in one of the farmers' houses when the AX rode up with the sheriff "

"Clarice!" Bob exclaimed. "I don't want yore name in this mess They can't make the murder charge stick. It takes a heap more evidence than a gunhawk's lies."

Jim Hatfield thoughtfully tugged at his chin He was recalling Matthews' statement that Bob Logsdon would stop a bullet if he managed to miss the hangnoose.

"I think Miss Hart's right," he said at last "Mebbe Tidy won't like knowin' about you and Clarice bein' together. But Tidy won't like the idea of an innocent gent bein' strung up for murder either. Don't you worry none about Tidy, Bob "

"But if I can beat the charge without her bein' in it?"

"You won't," Hatfield interrupted with a snap "Reynolds and Matthews know their case won't stand up, so they don't aim to let yuh come to trial I figger they've let yuh live this long hopin' yore farmer friends would try to break yuh out Once the farmers made a move like that they'd put theirselves clean outside the law, and Matthews could smash 'em That's what he wants "

"Yuh mean they'll salivate me right in this cell?" Bob demanded

"Why not?" Hatfield shot back "Yore pa was tended to quick and sudden Bars across an open window won't protect yuh from a bullet. Bob, Clarice better tell Tidy what she knows Once yuh're free, fan yore hoss home as fast as yuh can get there before a bushwhacker can reach yuh Yore friends will need all the fightin' men they can get before this is over "

Bob moved away from the window and Hatfield heard him pace back and forth in the small cell At last he reappeared at the window

"All right," he said reluctantly, "but it shore looks like I'm gettin' protection from a girl, and causin' a heap of talk about her "

"That doesn't worry me, Bob," Clarice said swiftly "It's your safety that counts. Father brought me to Matos. I'll tell him right away."

She moved swiftly away from the jail and Hatfield came to the window.

"Whatever yuh do," he warned, "get out of Matos before yuh stop a slug"

"Thanks, Geary," Bob said fervently. "Yuh're a man to ride the river with. Yuh'll keep in touch if anything happens?"

"Yuh can bank on that."

Hatfield faded into the shadows and worked his way to the street. He turned in at the Punchers' Rest. Kemper and Reynolds were at the bar and Hatfield joined them.

The lawman and the gunhawk were talking about the nesters and the rustling on the AX. Hatfield listened, wondering what had happened to Tidy and Clarice. The girl had had time enough to tell her story.

He heard quick, angry steps rap across the porch. The batwings burst open Matthews and Tidy Hart entered. The Deacon's long face was grim, two, angry red spots sat high on each cheek, and his eyes glittered

"Sheriff," he snapped, "Mr Hart has some new evidence about the Calvert killing"

"We got the gent that did it," Kemper said easily.

"Yuh got an innocent man!" Tidy shouted angrily. "Bob Logsdon and my daughter were together when Stumpy was shot They was nowheres near the place."

"What!" Kemper exclaimed and Reynolds looked swiftly at Matthews

Tidy nodded. "Clarice will swear to it and yore whole case against Bob Logsdon drops flat as yesterday's flapjack Yuh'd better get out yore keys, Kemper, and unlock that cell"

"I think Mr Hart is giving excellent advice," Matthews said carefully. "Miss Hart's evidence, of course, places a new light on the situation. Other steps can be taken. We'd better get over to the jail, Mr. Kemper."

Hatfield caught the swift flick of Matthews' angry eyes toward Reynolds The gunhawk blinked, then grinned crookedly, as the implication sank home. He followed Kemper out the batwings and Hatfield trailed after them.

Clarice Hart waited outside and Tidy ordered her to

come along with them to the jail In the sheriff's office she repeated her story, Matthews, Reynolds and Kemper watching her closely Jim Hatfield leaned against the wall, listening

"There it is," Matthews said when Clarice had finished. "Release Logsdon, Mr Kemper"

The sheriff reluctantly pulled his keys from his pocket and went into the cell block In a few minutes Bob Logsdon stepped into the office, blinking against the light. Reynolds narrowly eyed the young man, but Matthews managed to smile

"There has been a mistake, Logsdon," the AX manager said "You're free" His voice hardened "But AX has not forgotten that Stumpy Calvert was killed, and someone is going to pay for it"

"I've not forgotten either," Bob said quietly "I haven't forgot that I was positively identified as the killer—or that Pa was shot down right here in Matos There's a heap to be remembered, Mr Matthews Keep that in mind"

Bob Logsdon did exactly as Hatfield had ordered As soon as he left the jail he went directly to the livery stable, hired a horse, and left Matos before anyone could set a gun-trap for him From the porch of the Punchers' Rest, Hatfield watched the young farmer speed out of town, and breathed a sigh of relief He moved back to the batwings and peered over them into the lighted saloon

Tidy, Reynolds and Matthews sat in a close huddle at one of the back tables, arguing in low tones Tidy evidently was defending his daughter, and Bob Logsdon's release They would keep at it for some time.

Hatfield looked again toward the bank There was no light in Matthew's office, so Hatfield judged that when the man left the saloon he would go directly to his home

The Ranger moved down the steps and sauntered toward the bank, halted at the dark entrance to the stairway Except for lights in the two saloons, the town was dark Hatfield melted into the doorway, and felt his way up the stairs to Matthews' office. The door was locked, as he had expected, and he moved on down the dark hall toward a gray square of light that marked a window.

Silently he raised the sash and leaned out. The roof of a lean-to was just below him. In a moment the Ranger was on the lean-to and had closed the window behind him Moving along the brick wall, he came to a window of the ranch manager's office. It was closed and locked.

Suddenly he swung to one side and flattened himself against the wall when a light flared as the office door opened. Hatfield's hand dropped to his holster and the Colt was eased out as he stood tense and waiting The match flame died and another flared. A strong yellow glow came through the window as someone lighted a lamp.

Abruptly the lower window sash was raised and the light was partially blocked out as someone stood in the window less than two feet from the tense Ranger.

"Lock a place up for an hour and it's like an oven," Matthews said irritably.

He turned from the window, but Hatfield remained flat against the wall, head turned so he could hear what was being said in the room.

"Cuss Tidy's girl!" Reynolds snapped. "When we had everything figgered out "

"So we did," Matthews answered dryly Hatfield heard the swivel chair squeak as the man sat down "But things do go wrong at times We have to be prepared for them "

"Quit preachin'," Reynolds growled. "Bob Logsdon is loose again. That's the main point "

"Very much so," Deacon agreed.

There was a silence. Hatfield heard Reynolds pacing back and forth.

"Logsdon threw a heap of hints around when we let him go," Reynolds said. "He aims to cause trouble and plenty of it Stumpy Calvert and his pa stick in his craw and Bob won't let 'em drop. Yuh can depend on it."

"Certainly I do," Matthews snapped. "You should never have let him get out of town "

"He moved too blamed fast," grumbled Reynolds "By the time Tidy took his eyes off me, I had no chance to give an order. Bob'll hole up with them farmers and we won't get much of a chance at him."

"We have to," Deacon said quietly. "We stand to lose too much with Logsdon free and snooping around Reynolds, our job is just about done. It would be a shame not to be able to finish it."

"Yeah," Reynolds agreed heavily. "So far, Kemper has kept the lid on, no matter how much Tidy squawked. But it's been gettin' harder all along Them farmers are not goin' to obey a law badge much longer The Logsdons is the only ones that have ever had nerve enough to do anything, we took care of the old man, and we got to get Bob Logsdon somehow."

"Stumpy was killed by a rifle bullet," Deacon said thoughtfully. "It was good shooting I wonder if perhaps Bob Logsdon might not get another one of those rifle slugs"

"Risky," Reynolds said.

"Not if it's handled right," Deacon assured. "There are bushes along Matos Creek that border the fields They would hide a horse and a man He could use a telescope sight, do the job, and be gone before anyone would know"

"Mmm," Reynolds mused "Yeah, it could be done thataway Bob Logsdon is shore to be out lookin' over his farm to see what happened while he was in jail. I reckon it can be done."

"See to it," Matthews snapped "We've got to keep control for a while longer. The AX will drive off those farmers one way or another, and there's already a move to buy 'em out"

"Trimpe had that in mind," Reynolds chuckled.

"There's to be a new man down here before long with the same job to do," Matthews said. "Maybe the owners themselves I got a letter from Denver today. So take care of Logsdon We'll clean things up neat for the owners"

CHAPTER XII

Evidence

Jim Hatfield heard Reynolds open the door and leave the office But Matthews remained Hatfield listened, but apparently the ranch manager was seated in his chair, not moving At last he sighed deeply as though he had finished an unpleasant train of thought

He moved to the window and closed it. Shortly the light went out Hatfield remained motionless against the wall, until at last he felt certain he would not be discovered.

He moved to the window then, and found it locked. He wrapped his gun muzzle in his neckerchief and, with a single sharp blow, broke the glass just below the lock. He reached carefully through the jagged hole and in a few minutes silently pushed up the window and climbed into the dark office

Except for the one sharp blow, he had made no sound For minutes he stood beside the window, making sure there would be no alarm Then he pulled down the blind and felt his way to Matthews' desk He shielded a match with his hat, glanced around the room The desk, a file and a tall clothes cupboard were the only places where evidence might be hidden

Hatfield lighted the lamp, turned the wick low and set it on the floor so that no direct light would fall on the window blind, then started on the desk He worked efficiently, but found nothing incriminating Current ranch bills, catalogs, letters from buyers, and some notations in Matthews' angular hand. But all concerned the business of the AX.

It was the same story with the file, although the payrolls held him for a while and from them he discovered when the first of the gunhawks had been hired Letters about the farmers passing between Matthews and the

Denver representatives of the English owners threw little light on the subject. As Hatfield had suspected, Matthews had recommended violent ejection for the nesters.

As Hatfield opened the cupboard doors he saw a few old clothes hanging on racks. The bottom was bare.

Hatfield stepped back to the center of the room and looked around. He had searched every place and had found nothing that gave a clue to the killings and rustlings. Further investigation here was useless, and now he faced the problem of searching Matthews' home.

He had bent his head to blow out the lamp when his glance fell on the base of the cupboard. It was unusually high Hatfield's eyes narrowed and he bent down, rapping lightly on the wood that returned a hollow sound.

He began pushing and pulling at the knobby decorations that covered the base. He stumbled on the right combination and a section of the base slid back, revealing a dark hole.

Plunging his hand into the hole Hatfield's fingers struck the ridged binding of a thick ledger He pulled it out, held it close to the lamp and opened it Matthews' crabbed writing told a completely different story here.

There were records of cattle sold, notations of the price per head, and the total amount received. There was a list of names headed by that of Reynolds and, in fresh writing at the bottom, was the name of Tex Geary. Beside each name except Geary's, were small figures.

Another page was headed "Bank," and over a period of a year and a half the amount was impressive. Hatfield added this figure to the total in the columns beside the names and they equalled the sales price of the cattle shown at the beginning of the ledger.

He moved back to Matthews' desk and pulled out the regular ranch ledger. It showed no cattle sales on the dates in the ledger Hatfield had found. The ranger returned to the cupboard and closed the sliding panel. Holding the incriminating ledger, he considered what to do with it.

Part of his job was done and he felt a certain amount of elation. Matthews, despite his pious attitude, had been robbing his employers for a considerable time. The gun crew supposedly hired to protect the AX from farmer encroachment, actually ran off AX cattle.

The blame, of course, seemed to rest squarely on the farmers When they had moved in, Matthews' cunning brain had seen an opportunity to line his pockets at little risk to himself.

Hatfield replaced the lamp where he found it He looked around the room, making sure the desk and file were in order. Matthews would find the broken window and discover that the ledger was missing, but the Ranger wanted the man to believe it had been stolen by someone who knew exactly where it was, and had wasted no time getting it In this way, Hatfield warded off suspicion of himself

Satisfied that all was in order, Hatfield blew out the lamp, rolled up the blind and opened the window He stepped out onto the lean-to roof and moved silently to the low eaves It was a short drop to the ground and Hatfield landed silently He faded into the shadows, taking the ledger with him.

The book was too big to hide and its possession spelled death An idea came to Hatfield as he moved silently through the shadows, and he worked his way to the back of the blacksmith shop A few moments' prospecting around the ground and he found exactly what he needed, a piece of scrap metal that would serve as a crude spade.

Directly on line with the smithy was a cottonwood tree and Hatfield headed for it He started digging close to its roots and soon had a hole scooped out big enough to hide the book. He covered it in the wide neckerchief, then shoveled the dirt over it. He would have to return soon of course, with something that would give the incriminating ledger more protection in case of rain But the important thing now was to leave it where no one could find it

He stamped the earth down, threw the broken metal far out into the dark, grassy plain, then headed for the Punchers' Rest Reynolds and the other AX hands were still there

"Where yuh been?" Reynolds asked.

"Ridin'," drawled Hatfield. "I got plumb curious about what that Logsdon gent would do I trailed him quite a spell, but he headed right to Matos Creek"

"Cuss it!" Reynolds complained. "Wish I'd known what yuh was doin' Yuh could have finished up another little job for me. Too late now. We'd better head back toward the spread . . ."

Reynolds waited near the corral the next morning as the crew roped and saddled for the day's work. When Hatfield approached Reynolds gave him a slight signal and Hatfield followed him back to the empty bunkhouse. Reynolds sat down at one of the rickety tables. He picked up a pack of greasy cards and waved Hatfield to a seat.

"Yuh trailed Logsdon last night," he said thoughtfully, and aimlessly riffled the cards.

"Yeah, for several miles."

"He didn't savvy yuh was behind him?"

"None whatever," Hatfield answered readily Reynolds riffled the cards again, stared at one of the dirty windows.

"Reckon yuh could have salivated him easy, huh?"

"Might," Hatfield said. "But I don't care much for back-shootin'. I always like to give the other gent a taw for his iron"

"Shore." Reynolds nodded. He gave Hatfield a side-long look. "But suppose yuh didn't dare take that chance, Geary? Suppose yuh had to shut a gent up permanent and couldn't risk any mistakes?"

"Well,"—Hatfield hesitated—"that might be different. What's in yore craw, Reynolds?"

"A job for yuh, and yuh're just the man Yuh handle them sixes plumb fast and accurate. How about a rifle?"

"I reckon I'm all right"

"I thought so" Reynolds smiled crookedly "Geary, I'm givin' yuh a rifle with a telescope sight I want yuh to nail Bob Logsdon He'll work in his fields and yuh'll get a good chance at him from the bushes."

"Bushwhack?" Hatfield shook his head. "I told yuh how I feel about that"

"I heard yuh," Reynolds snapped. "But yuh're working

77

for me and for Deacon Matthews. We give orders, we expect 'em to be carried out But there's another side. We appreciate a gent who can do as he's told and do it right A gent like that gets a heap of extra dinero."

Hatfield traced a design with his fingernail on the table-top while Reynolds waited, sure of himself. Hatfield looked up, meeting Reynolds' searching glance.

"Yuh're sayin' if I turn this down, I'll run into trouble? If I take it, I get a bonus?"

"That's it," Reynolds answered. "Bonus or Boot Hill——yore choice If word comes that Logsdon's dead, yuh can expect some dinero the next day—plenty of it I'll give yuh three days to do the job."

Hatfield shrugged as if in hopeless surrender

"I reckon yuh've called the tally When do I start?"

A gunhawk suddenly appeared in the doorway and Reynolds jerked around angrily. The man hastly pointed outside with his thumb

"Deacon Matthews is here. He wants to see yuh right away"

"Comin'," Reynolds snapped He pushed up from the table "We'll finish our talk later. Hang around"

When he went out, Hatfield walked to the door and stood leaning against the post Matthews sat his horse, talking to Reynolds. Hatfield couldn't hear their conversation but could guess what it was about. Deacon Matthews looked worried, his questions appeared to be sharp.

Matthews had discovered the theft of the ledger. Reynolds looked blank, then began to scowl. His voice rose sharply so that Hatfield heard part of a sentence.

"—know nothin' about it."

The ranch manager swung out of the saddle, stood close to Reynolds for a while Hatfield moved back and sat down at the table. In a few minutes Matthews and Reynolds came in.

Hatfield quickly sensed that neither of the two men knew exactly what to say.

Matthews sank down in a chair, considered his thumbnail for a moment.

"Geary," he asked then, "what did you do after Bob Logsdon was released?"

"Why, I told Reynolds—" Hatfield began, but Matthews interrupted him with a quick gesture.

"You're telling me now, Geary."

Hatfield looked from one to the other, acting the part of a man who is surprised and puzzled.

"Why, I left the jail and loafed back toward the Punchers' Rest," he said. "I was on the porch when I saw Logsdon ride out of town mighty fast and I figgered mebbe you or Reynolds would like to know where he went I trailed him for a space, then rode back "

"Very commendable." Matthews nodded and glanced swiftly at Reynolds. "When you came back to Matos, what did you do?"

"I went to the Punchers' Rest and told Reynolds what the farmer had done "

"You went directly to the saloon? Nowhere else?"

"Shore," Hatfield answered, his mouth suddenly grim. "Anything wrong with what I did? Why are yuh askin' all these questions?"

"Nothing wrong," Matthews hastily assured, "and you used your head to trail Bob Logsdon. By the way, did you see any of the AX crew outside the saloon when you rode back?"

"No," Hatfield answered flatly.

"Yuh know where Matthews' office is?" Reynolds asked sharply.

Hatfield stared at him blankly.

"Shore You took me there. It's up over the bank. I see a place once, I remember it."

"I'm sure you do, Geary," Matthews said, with a smile.

He arose and walked to the door, Reynolds following him The ranch manager turned slowly and again used his unctuous smile and voice.

"Don't mention this little talk to anyone else, Geary. It's just between us. You, Reynolds and myself "

CHAPTER XIII

Bushwhack Job

When Matthews and Reynolds were gone, Jim Hatfield spread his long legs under the table. He felt sure he would not be questioned again about the missing ledger. Matthews was uncertain as to who might have committed the theft, but he must be certain that someone familiar with the office had done the job. Matthews' attention would center on the older hands, might even turn to Reynolds himself.

Hatfield hoped that the new development would cancel the orders for the Logsdon killing. Once that job was definitely handed to him, the Ranger's masquerade at the AX was over. Even if he did not disclose his identity, he would be definitely lined on the side of the farmers.

Hatfield lifted his head when he heard Tidy Hart's angry voice raised in the yard. Reynolds bellowed something, then Matthews' soft voice cut in. Hatfield slipped to the door. Tidy, Matthews and Reynolds stood before the cookshack.

Reynolds' hand hovered above his holstered six. Tidy looked like a fighting bantam beside him, and fairly trembled from head to toe. Matthews' face was pinched, his eyes glittering.

"I'm manager of the AX," Hatfield heard him say flatly. "You may have a pull with the owners, Mr. Hart, but I still give orders."

"Then yuh'd better wake up to what's happenin'," Tidy snapped. "The AX is overloaded with men like Reynolds and his gunslammin' breed. We're losin' beef steady. I've reported it to yuh time and again and yuh say yuh've passed the word on to the owners. Why don't they do somethin' about it?"

"They have, Mr. Hart," Matthews answered. "Sheriff Kemper is investigating. I've hired Mr. Reynolds and other men who can protect the ranch from depredations "

"Kemper!" Tidy exploded. "That—that trained puppy of yores! I've seen a heap better lawman in an Injun village! Gunhawks protect us? Fiddlesticks! There's been more killin' and thievin' since they came than ever before. You blame it on the nesters, but I ain't so shore We had no cattle stealin' till Reynolds and his gang came."

"Meaning?" Reynolds demanded

Hatfield straightened, ready to take a hand to protect the fiery little segundo.

Tidy glared at Reynolds. "Meanin' I ain't so shore of you and yore crew Matthews, what yuh aim to do about it?"

"Exactly what I've done before," Matthews answered coldly "I'm competent to judge what's best, Mr. Hart. Here and now you have orders to let me handle this as I see fit "

"Then here and now, yuh got my resignation!" Tidy flared "I'm loyal to the AX and I aim to do what's best If yuh won't ask the Texas Rangers to step into this mess of killin', rustlin' and nesters, then I will! Yuh can't stop me "

"Yuh're mighty shore of that," Reynolds said threateningly, but subsided when Matthews shook his head.

"You had better reconsider this, Mr Hart," the ranch manager said "Why are you so suddenly determined to call in the Rangers? Do you have new information?"

Hatfield realized now that Matthews believed Tidy had stolen the incriminating ledger The little segundo's revolt and demand for the Rangers had been badly timed. Hatfield caught the swift look that passed between Matthews and Reynolds.

"I have the same information," Tidy snapped, "that you have It's enough to call in the Rangers and you know it! I hate to leave the AX, but if that's what it takes to get this range straightened up, I'll leave. How about it, Matthews?"

"Kemper is sufficient law for me," Matthews said stiffly.

"Then get yoreself a new segundo," said Tidy. "I've

81

plumb quit—but yuh ain't heard the last of me by a long sight."

He turned on his heel and strode angrily toward the ranchhouse.

Hatfield tensed, his fingers taloning over his Colts, for Reynolds' hand had dropped to his holster But Matthews caught his wrist. Matthews spoke swiftly to the gunhawk, and at last Reynolds growled angrily and shrugged Neither of the three men had been aware that Hatfield had been a witness to the encounter.

The Ranger knew that Tidy Hart had signed his own death warrant when he resigned from the AX. Matthews and Reynolds could not allow the man to leave the district, and Tidy's threat to call in the Rangers was pure dynamite. Hatfield also knew now that the absentee owners were not sure of their ranch manager, since Matthews apparently did not know that his employers had already placed an appeal with the great law enforcement body.

Reynolds came into the bunkhouse and strode up to the table where Hatfield was sitting again. The gunhawk was breathing hard as though he had run a race, and in his eyes was a malevolent glitter.

"Yore job's been changed," he said shortly. "Yuh won't need a rifle this time. Saddle up and loosen yore sixes. Yuh'll use 'em"

"On who?" Hatfield asked.

"Tidy Hart and his girl will be ridin' to Matos shortly," Reynolds said. "Tidy's bucked the Deacon and nobody gets away with that Yuh're to see that neither of 'em get far."

"The girl, too?" Hatfield asked.

"She can talk as much as her pa," Reynolds growled. "Yuh'll get a thousand dollars if the job is done right—a lead slug if yuh fail. On yore way, pronto. Pick yore place and be ready when Tidy comes along They'll probably be in the buckboard. Bring it back to the spread"

"But—"

"No arguments," barked Reynolds "I'll take care of you and all the details. Hit the saddle—pronto.

82

Hatfield shrugged and arose He went to the corral, saddled Goldy, and rode away toward Matos The AX spread finally dropped out of sight behind him and Hatfield drew rein, eyes thoughtful and hard chin set as he considered what to do Suddenly his face lighted and his lips spread in a wide smile. He touched Goldy lightly with blunt spurs and rode on until he came to a cottonwood There he dismounted and made himself comfortable for a long wait.

Almost two hours passed before Hatfield saw the buckboard in which Tidy and Clarice road approaching Hatfield arose, swung into the saddle, and trotted out from the shade of the cottonwood

Instantly Tidy pulled up the buckboard and bent swiftly down Hatfield caught the glint of metal as the man lifted a rifle. Clarice tried to check him, but Tidy threw off her arm

Hatfield lifted his hands high and slowed Goldy's pace to an ambling walk Tidy held the rifle steady and Hatfield saw the determined gleam in the man's eyes. Tidy's white imperial fairly trembled in anger.

"What do you want, Geary?" he challenged.

"Palaver," Hatfield said quietly. Using his knees, he halted Goldy a few feet away

"Yuh been sent to salivate me," Tidy accused.

"That's right " Hatfield nodded and Tidy's eyes opened wide in surprise The Ranger nodded to the girl. "She'll tell yuh where I stand "

"He's a friend, Dad," Clarice said swiftly. "I've tried to tell you so "

"Any hombre of Reynolds' gun crew is a lyin' skunk and a treacherous yeller dog!" Tidy exploded

Hatfield's gentle smile didn't lessen, and he nodded again.

"Yuh're right Have Miss Clarice lift my guns, Tidy, and yuh can keep that rifle right on my brisket. I want to palaver and my arms are getting mighty tired stuck up in the air like this."

Tidy glared at him for a moment in silence Then he ordered Clarice to get the guns. She climbed from the buckboard and approached Hatfield with a smile. She lifted the Colt from one holster, circled the horse and took the other She walked back to the buckboard and Hatfield lowered his arms with a relieved sigh. Tidy's rifle didn't waver.

"Start yore palaver," he said coldly.

"I'm reachin' in my clothes for somethin' yuh'll want to see," Hatfield said "So don't get too blamed nervous with that rifle trigger. Yuh'll know why I'm workin' on the AX"

Slowly he lifted the badge from its secret pocket. He held it out so that Tidy could see the glittering. star inside the metallic circle. Tidy's jaw dropped, and Clarice gasped

"Ranger!" Tidy whispered. "But yuh're—"

"Apparently workin' for Reynolds" Hatfield nodded. "I posed as a gent from the Big Bend with guns for hire and Reynolds took the bait, Hart The owners of the AX sent us a letter askin' us to investigate conditions here They sent it none too soon"

Tidy lowered the rifle.

"Why didn't yuh give me some sign or let me know who yuh was?"

"Because I didn't dare tip my hand to anyone I had to find out about the Matos Range and who fought whom I had to know where the nesters fitted in, and get some line on the rustlin's As far as I could know, any one of yuh might have done some of the killin' around here"

"Then yuh know what's goin' on." Tidy sighed in relief His eyes sparkled with new life. "Yuh know what Matthews has done to ruin the AX and how we been losin' beefs Yuh know how them renegades keep the nesters stirred up to 'suit their own purpose despite the fact that Brant Trimpe wanted to buy 'em out peaceful"

"I know a heap," Hatfield answered "But I ain't got all the picture. For instance, what about Trimpe? Did you see the shootin'?"

"No." Tidy shook his head. "It happened in the bunk-house"

"Who was with him?"

"Deacon Matthews. Trimpe was to do a little huntin'.

Deacon claimed it was accidental and I shore couldn't say one way or the other Mebbe it was, though Deacon ain't above a little fancy killin', for all his nice talk"

"No proof though." Hatfield frowned. "I want to pin these murders on the killers Right now I can stop the rustlin'. That's important, but it's not the whole job. I've got to stay on the AX as Tex Geary, gunslammer. I've been ordered to get rid of you and Miss Hart"

Tidy's chin thrust out.

"Reynolds and Matthews again. How yuh goin' to get around the job?"

"With yore help," Hatfield answered readily. "Yuh're not ridin' to Matos We'll head for Bob Logsdon's place and yuh'll hole- up there till I give yuh the word. I'll bring the buckboard and team back to the AX with mebbe some chicken or beef blood on it, and that'll satisfy Reynolds for a while

"Logsdon!" Tidy exclaimed.

"I saw Ray Logsdon shot," Hatfield said, "and Reynolds is due for arrest on that killin' alone. Bob is straight and honest He'll see yuh're protected and he'll meet a reasonable offer from the AX owners more'n halfway. Let's head for Matos Creek right away, Hart. We might be seen"

Just at sundown Hatfield came back to the AX. He rode in the buckboard, Goldy trotting along behind As he wheeled into the yard, Reynolds came swaggering out of the ranchhouse The gunhawk's face lighted.

"Seems like yuh done a job, Geary," he said

Hatfield nodded, and bent down and picked up Clarice's bonnet and Tidy's Stetson.

"Figured yuh might-like to see these. We can get rid of 'em when I wash these bloodstains off the buckboard. I don't think anyone will find the bodies."

Reynolds laughed and nodded

"Plumb missin', huh? Just as well By the way, I'm the new AX segundo I don't reckon we'll be bothered much with snoopers on our own spread any more. From now on we rule the roost."

"How about Logsdon?" Hatfield inquired

"Forget it," Reynolds said "We got other plans."

CHAPTER XIV

Surprise Visit

Peace reigned on the Matos range for the next week With the going of Tidy Hart, Matthews and Reynolds immediately took over the AX One by one, the regular punchers were fired, or life was made so unpleasant for them that they saddled up and drifted.

A few gunhawks drifted in to take their places, and the AX was almost completely an outlaw spread

Matthews and Reynolds tore the house apart in a futile search for the missing ledger. There was not a corner, a possible hiding place that they did not ransack.

Though the ledger had not yet been discovered Matthews controlled the only law in Matos, so if this incriminating evidence were turned over to Sheriff Kemper it would immediately reach Matthews' hands But Matthews believed that, even if it had been sent to the Rangers, he still had sufficient time to carry out his plans before anyone could interfere.

During the period of reorganization of the AX spread, Reynolds made no moves against the nesters, nor did he run off any more AX beef But Hatfield could plainly see that both moves were coming.

On two nights he rode to Matos with the men Their swagger was pronounced now, as though already they considered this whole range their own. There was no news whatsoever about the farmers along Matos Creek.

Hatfield was pleased about that, for it meant that Bob Logsdon maintained good control of his men So long as their silence continued, Tidy and Clarice would be safe —and Hatfield would not be suspected. On one of the nights in the town, Hatfield managed to slip away and dig up Matthews' ledger. He replaced the neckerchief with an old poncho, wrapping it so that no moisture would reach the pages and blot the evidence. Replaced in its hiding place it would now be safe until such time as it was needed

With only their own kind on the ranch, the gunhawks became more free in their talk Hatfield learned enough to throw three-fourths the crew in jail

There were guarded allusions to some of the AX killings and Hatfield learned definitely that only Tidy Hart's men had been done away with Meacham confirmed this one night as he and Hatfield talked out by the corral

"I reckon Stumpy was the last of the old crew we had to salivate," he said "Looked at first like we was goin' to have to knock 'em off one by one, risky as that was."

"So that's the way yuh worked it," Hatfield marveled.

Meacham chuckled "Shore—blamin' it and the rustlin' on them nesters Kemper would do just as Matthews said Like the time I plugged the hoss wrangler, Kelly. Kemper had an idea it was me, but he didn't let on."

"Blamed obligin' lawman," Hatfield grunted.

"Oh, Kemper gets his cut right along," Meacham said off-handedly

As Hatfield walked to the bunkhouse with Meacham, to turn in, he knew that he could now bring one of the killers to justice and he had a line on the crooked sheriff There remained the mystery of Stumpy Clavert's and Brant Trimpe's deaths

Hatfield fairly ached to throw off his disguise immediately and place the whole AX crew under arrest.

Early the next morning, on his way to the cookshack, Hatfield saw a rider come in from Matos. He dismounted in the yard and strode to the ranchouse Minutes later Reynolds came bursting into the cookshack The crew sensed his excitement and talk 'died down. Reynolds looked them over, grinning crookedly.

"You killin' sons is goin' to have to act like nice woolly lambs the next week," he announced. "The English owners are in Matos and they'll be out here this afternoon. They're goin' to stay for a while and look over their property" Abruptly Reynolds stopped smiling "We didn't expect these gents and they can shore upset our plans if they get any idea what's goin' on"

87

"Salivate 'em," Meacham suggested, and Reynolds wheeled around angrily.

"Not these hombres. They're dukes or somethin' and if anything happened to 'em, we'd have the place crawlin' with lawmen and Rangers No, yuh just got to keep yore lips buttoned If they ask questions, answer so's they won't get suspicious. Savvy?"

The men nodded and Reynolds went on briskly.

"We got to clean up the place. It's got to look like a mighty prosperous ranch, not an owlhooters' camp It's got to be done by this afternoon so there ain't goin' to be no loafin'" He named off some to clean out the bunkhouse and cookshack. Others were to straighten up the ranchouse, and another crew was set at work on the yard and barns Under Reynolds' watchful and threatening eye the ranch changed miraculously. It fairly glittered by the time a buggy appeared on the Matos road

As the buggy rolled up and stopped, Hatfield sauntered with the rest of the outfit to form a curious circle around the vehicle Deacon Matthews stepped out, followed by two tall men dressed in expensive, but baggy tweeds

One of them fumbled with a black cord, then placed a monocle in his eye. He was florid, fair-haired, and had a long straight nose. Disregarding the monocle, Hatfield read courage and breeding in the man's clear blue eyes.

"I say, this is quite a ranch, what!" the Englishman said to Matthews.

"Mighty big, your lordship," Matthews said, bobbing his head He asked the other Englishman "What do you think of Texas, Mr Montague?"

"I hardly know," the Briton replied

He was a touch shorter than his companion His skin was deeply tanned as though a tropical sun had scorched it for years. His shoulders were square, his back stiff, as though it had not been long before that he had worn a uniform and commanded men. A scar from a saber cut lay along one lean cheek

Matthews faced the crew.

"Boys, I want you to meet your real bosses—Lord Ramsden, and Mr. Montague They've come from London to pay us a visit and see how we're getting along I want you to do all you can to make them comfortable."

"We'll shore do that," Reynolds promised for the men He nodded toward the house. "We got yore place all fixed up for yuh"

The Englishmen murmured their thanks and entered the house Matthews and Reynolds followed them Their luggage was eagerly lifted out and placed on the porch where another man picked up the bags and took them inside.

Hatfield went back to the bunkhouse with the rest of the men There were ribald remarks about the Englishmen, broad and crude imitations of their mannerisms and speech Hatfield sat quietly on his bunk, watching without really seeing He was weighing the advisability of a direct report to Montague and Lord Ramsden.

They should know the condition of their own spread, but the Ranger doubted if that would help his case. Ramsden would probably insist on the instant dismissal and arrest of Matthews and Reynolds, something Hatfield wanted to avoid for a while. Montague might be more open to suggestion.

One other factor influenced Hatfield's decision. If the two Englishmen knew of trouble on the AX, they would not leave until it had been settled. Their presence would check Matthews' plans, probably arouse suspicion in the manager's mind that his employers suspected something

That might lead to a double killing and flight out of Texas Hatfield didn't want to run that risk As it stood, Matthews was skating on thin ice. Hatfield decided to let events shape themselves.

"Geary!" Reynolds called from the bunkhouse doorway.

Hatfield walked over to him, and Reynolds silently led the way to the big barn. Inside it, Reynolds threw a quick glance at the ranchhouse.

"How fast can yuh chouse along a bunch of beefs?" he asked abruptly.

Hatfield showed his surprise "Fast enough, I reckon, given the right men to work with. I can make 'em sprout wings if there's lead flyin'."

"That's just how fast yuh got to drive this time," Reynolds said. "Them two English gents didn't come out here for a vacation They want to see the books, look over-the spread, and make a tally of the beefs"

"Owners' privilege," Hatfield murmured, and Reynolds grunted in angry disgust.

"Shore, but yuh don't think we've been workin' for punchers' wages, do yuh? All of us have made dinero from AX beef Matthews has showed some losses on the books, but not near enough to cover what we've drove off toward Palo Duro, sold, and divided."

"Didn't expect 'em?" Hatfield asked

"Cuss it, no! Who'd figger a couple of gents would come clear from England to count a bunch of whitefaces? They handled things through a Denver business office, and the Denver men accepted Matthews' reports and the ledger he kept."

"Looks like yuh're in a tight," Hatfield shrugged "You can't bushwhack the Englishmen and yuh can't let 'em take a tally."

Reynolds laughed and a look of cunning passed over his face

"I think we can, Geary—take a tally, I mean—if you do yore part The next two days Montague and Ramsden are ridin' over AX range The follerin' day, they're takin' a tally. We got enough beefs left to string 'em out considerable Now if they was run in a big circle, a man that didn't know, would count the same cows over and over again, You'll have the men, Can yuh do it?"

"I can," Hatfield answered.

Reynolds laughed and nudged the Ranger's ribs with his elbow

"Then we're safe enough At least long enough to satisfy these two gents so's we can make a final clean-up after they've gone"

"Then what?" Hatfield asked.

"Just pull stakes," Reynolds answered, "and leave the AX high and dry The Englishmen can do what they blame well please with a big range that won't have a cow on it. Yuh'll get more detailed orders about the tally before we start, Geary. I'll tell Deacon yuh'll do the job."

Reynolds grinned again and walked away from the barn. Hatfield watched him go with a certain amount of grudging admiration This gunhawk and his sly partner had a great deal of courage and boldness, though directed to evil purposes The average crook in their position would have fled without a moment's delay at the coming of the Englishmen for a thorough audit and count These two planned a bold play that promised to work through sheer audacity.

Hatfield shook his head regretfully. If only this same audacity and intelligence had been used constructively, the Matos range would probably be the richest in all of Texas.

CHAPTER XV

Final Plans

Lord Ramsden and Mr Montague first inspected the buildings of the ranch. They were everywhere, asking innumerable questions, but Matthews or Reynolds was always with them. They seemed pleased with the buildings and their cleanliness.

Hatfield was present in the corral when the question of the change in the crew came up

"It's really very strange," Lord Ramsden said, "that for years we've had the same men on the payroll, and now they're all gone Within the last year Can't quite understand it, you know "

"Range trouble mostly," Matthews said easily. "Those nesters settled on open range, land that was granted as subsidy to the railroads The farmers bought title and the AX was caught short We tried to get them off, but they're a lawless bunch. There have been killings "

"Then these new hands won't last long?" Montague asked.

"These men will stick," Matthews said grimly "I've hand picked them for trouble. You have a fighting crew on the AX now "

Montague's hands were clasped behind his back, his powerful legs spread. He gave Hatfield an impression of power

"I can't understand this farmer problem," he said "We gave orders that they were to be bought out peacefully Mr. Trimpe, unfortunately, was killed and the deal fell through. However, it's deucedly strange that the farmers should resort to violence "

"Just land-greedy, I reckon." Matthews shrugged "If they could acquire more land for farming, driving out the AX, this whole range would be farming country "

"Mmm," Montague said thoughtfully. "I think we

should have a talk with these farmers—appeal for fair play, y'know."

Matthews couldn't conceal the fear that flicked over his face. Hatfield saw Montague's eyes narrow, but the Briton said nothing.

Matthews shook his head.

"Mr. Montague," he said, "you and Lord Ramsden would run considerable risk "

"I'm not a stranger to risk," Montague snapped. "I've campaigned in Africa and India, y'know—Royal Leicester Rifles. I don't believe a Texas bullet is more dangerous than a Zulu spear or an Afghan musket ball."

Matthews stubbornly shook his head. "I've got your safety to think about. I'll try to arrange the meeting, of course, but I'll have to be the judge if it's safe. I couldn't explain your deaths."

The party moved on to the bunkhouse, leaving Hatfield alone, currying Goldy's smooth, satiny coat. He knew that word of the presence of the Englishmen had surely spread over the neighborhood Tidy Hart and Bob Logsdon would both be eager to contact the AX owners, and the Ranger did not want them to make the try. It would mean running the risk of their deaths, and of upsetting Hatfield's plans.

He saddled and rode away from the ranch. No one paid much attention to him. After he was out of sight of the buildings, Hatfield turned Goldy, making a wide circle around the AX and heading for the farms along Matos Creek.

He approached carefully, not knowing what to expect if someone other than Bob Logsdon spied him Luckily, the young farmer was working close to the fence in his fields. Bob spotted the rider some distance off and waited, rifle ready, until he saw that his visitor was Hatfield He came to the fence.

"Howdy, Ranger," he greeted, with a wide grin "Clarice told me who yuh are and it shore was good news."

"Yuh got 'em safe hid?" Hatfield asked.

Bob Logsdon nodded. "Shore—but Tidy's about to bust a hamstring. He don't like hidin'. Claims he's goin' to palaver with the owners that's come."

"I was afraid of that," Hatfield said grimly. "Tell him he's to keep under cover. Neither of yuh are to make any move to reach them Englishmen' Reynolds' gunhawks would blast yuh down in a minute."

"But we got to present our side," Bob protested

"I know yore side and I'll back yuh when the time comes Bob, yuh'd not even reach the Englishmen Every AX gunhawk would try his blamedest to cut yuh down on sight Same with Tidy I told Reynolds I took care of him and Miss Hart Suppose he shows up all of a sudden? What happens to me?"

Bob was silent and at last he nodded.

"I see yore point. But, Ranger, we can't keep up this hidin' much longer Something's got to break "

"It will," Hatfield promised. "Mebbe sooner than yuh think"

Hatfield rode back to the ranch, to find Reynolds impatiently waiting for him Montague and Lord Ramsden had decided to count the cattle the next day and the roundup crew had already spread out across the range. Reynolds had some explicit directions to give Hatfield and he inserted a few rather blunt warnings about failure.

When Hatfield awoke the next morning there was an air of tension about the ranch. The Englishmen had not appeared, but Matthews and Reynolds were in the cookshack, giving last-minute orders and checking the whole scheme The owners had to be completely fooled or this lucrative game would come to an untimely end by sundown.

"All right" Reynolds straightened after a long talk. "Geary, take yore crew down beyond the barn The boys will chouse the cows yore way. You know what to do after that "

Hatfield nodded.

The corrals were covered with billowing dust Ropes snaked in to capture mounts. Men cursed as they cinched saddles and rode the hump out of their mounts' backs Goldy came trotting up at Hatfield's shrill whistle, and in a short time he rode out beyond the barn with half a dozen hardcases.

94

Montague and Ramsden came out on the porch and Matthews hurried to meet them. The two Englishmen took their posts out by the winter feed bins. They faced one another over a wide expanse of hard-packed, bare ground, each with a pad of tally sheets.

Matthews stood behind Montague, while Reynolds acted as checker for Lord Ramsden. The Englishmen were a little nervous, Hatfield could see. This was a job they had never done before.

At Matthews' signal, a man streaked out beyond the barn to the holding pasture. All the AX cattle were there. At first glance it looked to be an immense herd, but it was pitifully small compared to what the AX range had once grazed. With shrill yips and yells the punchers started the herd forward. Hatfield's men waited for their turn

The first of the cattle headed for the barn at a dead run. They came fast, well strung out, but still a sizable bunch. Hatfield and his men rode out to meet them, turned the corner of the barn and into the sight of the Englishmen Hatfield kept the cows moving fast, heading the lead steer directly down the center of the bare strip between the counters. The rest of the herd thundered behind him.

Dust rose in choking clouds. Hatfield hung to the side of the lead steer. He streaked by the counters and, when he judged himself well clear of the feeding pens, turned the lead steer. Instantly the buildings cut him off from the sight of the owners.

Constantly turning the lead animal, Hatfield headed him back toward the pasture. Not far ahead, the last of the herd raced toward the barn, the feeding stalls, and the counters. A sweating puncher took Hatfield's place, with a crooked grin showing through the stubble.

"Shore a merry-go-round!" he shouted above the noise, and Hatfield raised his hand in acknowledgment as he turned Goldy away from the cattle.

He headed toward the barn, sharply watching the herd and the way the men handled them Matthews was taking a bold chance, simply herding the same bunch of cattle around and around the spread to be counted again and again. Hatfield wondered if the Englishmen had any suspicion of the trick that was being played on them.

He waited by the barn, saw that every man did his job. Then he swung in with the herd and rode to the checkers. Everything was dust, bawling cattle, noise and confusion Hatfield pulled up beside Montague and nodded a silent answer to Matthews' harried, questioning look.

Montague sweated, tried to squint through the dust. Cattle passed like black hurtling shadows.

"Tally—six hundred!" Matthews called loudly.

"Six hundred—check!" came Reynolds' voice.

Montague looked flustered He made a hasty correction on his tally sheet and the count continued.

Matthews would call the tally, in the confusion making twenty or thirty head count for fifty or more. Reynolds would instantly confirm the padded figure with a check call.

The two Englishmen were helpless Cattle streamed before them and they did not have the practised eyes to count them accurately Matthews' count and Reynolds' instant check added to their confusion. Unwilling to acknowledge that they were hopelessly lost, Montague and Lord Ramsden accepted the count, correcting their own uncertain tally at each call.

Matthews twisted around in the saddle and made a swift sign to Hatfield Instantly he neck-reined Goldy and headed for the pasture. He gave orders to the men to hold the beefs on the next round, and raced back to the feed stalls

The cattle streamed by, then stopped coming Montague wearily shoved his pencil in his shirt pocket and worked his aching fingers. Matthews looked up at the sun.

"Better knock off for food, I reckon. That's about half of the beefs"

"The rest?" Montague asked.

"We're running them up from the outlying pastures," Matthews lied easily. "We can start the count this afternoon."

"What about the cattle already tabulated?" Montague asked.

"We pushed them on out on the range to make room for the other herds coming in," Matthews said "Better check your tally with Lord Ramsden at dinner We can balance any little differences you might have before we start the second count "

"Deucedly fast work," Montague said, and moved off. Matthews swung in behind him, with a quick look of triumph toward Hatfield

The renegade crew was elated that they had so easily fooled the Englishmen But there was still a certain amount of tension among them as they wolfed the noon meal There could still be slips

But there were none. In the afternoon the herd again passed before the Englishmen and they made their useless tallies At last Matthews gave the signal that the farce was to be ended, and Hatfield broke the huge circle by heading the lead steer off toward the distant range

Dust clouds slowly settled, turned into a golden-red haze by the long sun rays. Montague and Lord Ramsden turned wearily toward the house

Hatfield stretched out in his bunk after the evening meal. There was not much talk among the men, for they were too tired Hatfield judged that probably the herd contained little more than six hundred head of cattle, yet the tally had run into thousands That told the Ranger the amount of the thefts that had been made

Hatfield drifted off to sleep, still marveling at the brazen boldness Matthews had displayed

CHAPTER XVI

First Arrests

Matthews ordered Hatfield to ride with the buggy to Matos the next morning There the Englishmen conferred in Matthews' office for a short time Their tally checked with the beef count as shown in the ranch records that Matthews had falsified

Montague and Lord Ramsden put their signatures to the cattle count and approved the ranch books The crooked ranch manager had gained more time in which to make the final steal

Hatfield drove the visitors to the distant railroad station They were tired, apparently glad to leave Texas For miles Hatfield debated whether to disclose his identity and tell them the truth about matters He came close to it when Montague shifted restlessly and sighed

"Deuced glad it's over," he said to Lord Ramsden

"So am I," Ramsden answered "We can report that the AX is under good management. We won't need to be suspicious any more of the changes that have been made I'm quite satisfied with Mr. Matthews His statements were clear and concise"

"Enlightening, what!" Montague said wearily "Might be best if we wrote to these Ranger people again, y'know There's no need for them to take a hand"

"Jove, you're right!" Ramsden exclaimed "We'll send a telegram. I say, aren't these Rangers supposed to be top-hole? Seems as though they take a long time to get around to answering our request I thought the place would fairly be swarming with bobbies"

"No matter. We're calling them off"

Hatfield had to check a strong impulse to reveal himself there and then But his better judgment prevailed Matthews and Reynolds would not hesitate to kill in order to make their escape, and the lives of these two men would be endangered if Hatfield disclosed the true state of the ranch His jaw tightened and he sat stonily staring out over the wide expanse of grass

They reached the railroad station late in the afternoon. The Englishmen filed their telegram to the Rangers Hatfield saw them board the train, but when it pulled out, he strode to the station

"Got yore job on AX I see," the station master said.

Hatfield nodded, picked up a pad of blanks and started writing a message He explained briefly the trick Matthews had pulled on the tally, the progress of the case to date. He asked Captain McDowell to contact the owners at Denver, asking them to sit tight until arrests had been made

He shoved the message to the man behind the counter. As the station master read it, his jaw dropped He looked up, staring

"Ranger, huh! This sounds like yuh shore uncovered something"

Hatfield displayed his badge and his gray-green eyes locked with those of the station master

"Any loose talk now is dangerous—to me, and to the case Yuh'll get yourself in serious trouble if yuh spread any rumors"

"Love yuh, man, I ain't got no such intention a-tall I like a peaceful range and it's worried me because AX shipments dropped off so much. Don't worry none about me, Ranger I'm for yuh"

Hatfield smiled, returned to the buggy and started the long trip back to Matos He arrived after dark and stopped at the Punchers' Rest Matthews, Reynolds and some of the gun crew were there, celebrating the departure of their bosses Matthews called Hatfield over to his table

"Our friends are safely on their way?" Matthews asked.

"Miles along by now," Hatfield answered

Matthews chuckled and rubbed his bony hands together.

"They didn't mention their visit, did they?"

"Some Seems like them gents wasn't exactly sure about you, Matthews, when they come. Plumb satisfied now, though. They was regretful about Tidy Hart ridin' off like he did Seems he had a job on the AX as long as he lived."

"Too bad," Matthews said, with a malicious grin

He pulled a wallet from his pocket, counted out greenbacks into a pile before Hatfield

"That's for that Hart job, and two hundred more for the way you handled the cattle "

"Thanks," Hatfield said dryly, picked up the money and placed it in his pocket.

Matthews hitched forward, and his voice dropped.

"We're about ready for our last play, Geary We want to cover it, so we're going to stir up the nesters They'll be shooting mad, and start a range war. While folks are worrying about it, we'll run the cattle to Palo Duro and make a getaway as slick as a whistle "

"Then what?" Hatfield demanded

Matthews laughed. "For me, Reynolds and you, there'll be other jobs I like your way of handling things, Geary. We'll find something in New Mexico that'll make us easy money "

"Sounds good, but what yuh plan next for the AX?"

"We're going to start fencing," Matthews said. "We're going to string wire all around the Matos Creek farms, cut them off from the town You can figure what'll happen "

"Trouble," Hatfield answered shortly "They'll cut the wire "

"No I'm assigning a bunch of the boys to you, Geary. You'll patrol the wire, see that our fencing crews aren't jumped while they're setting the posts and stringing the barbs Fact is"—Matthews smiled—"I want you to ask for trouble."

So Matthews had planned the showdown The farmers would have to fight through the fence and the patrols the AX would throw around them There would be gunsmoke, accusations Kemper would make arrests, the whole countryside would be in an uproar Under cover of that, the renegades would strip the AX of the last of its wealth and disappear into New Mexico

100

By the time word got to Denver, Matthews and Reynolds would be hard to find

Matthews nodded pleasantly "A neat ending to an involved piece of business, Geary There is just one other item I wish to bring forcefully to your attention It would be best all around if Bob Logsdon were dead, not only for my sake but for yours"

"I'll try for him," Hatfield said

"We start setting posts tomorrow," Matthews said "So you can be ready for gunsmoke ."

The next morning a wagon lumbered out from the AX spread and the driver headed for Matos Creek Around him rode some of the hardcase crew who seemed fairly to ache for trouble

Ahead of the group, Hatfield rode beside Reynolds. The segundo chuckled aloud

"This blows things wide apart, Geary There ain't much chance of us losin' a pot from now on."

The Ranger grinned, but Reynolds failed to see that the smile did not extend to the gray-green eyes. For Hatfield knew that he now could number the hours to the end of his masquerade on the AX Once the building of the fence was begun, Bob Logsdon would not be able to hold the farmers in check It would take someone with far more authority than the young nester, and that meant Jim Hatfield

As he rode beside Reynolds, Hatfield planned his next moves Meacham was in the crowd around the wagon and Meacham had confessed to one of the AX killings, and claimed to know about others The man had sided Reynolds when Ray Logsdon had been shot down and evidently was in the segundo's confidence Hatfield's jaw set

When the cultivated fields could be seen, Reynolds held up his hand and the little cavalcade stopped.

"We'll start setting 'em here," the segundo ordered. "We'll border the creek, swing clean around it and parallel this row on the other side, cut back across the creek and close the fence. Keep yore posts on AX property. We want to be plumb legal Wire's comin' behind yuh and it'll start goin' up in an hour after the first posts is set Geary, yuh can start yore job "

"I'll scout the farms first," Hatfield said "I'll need only one man for that More, when the nesters start fightin' the fence I'll take Meacham with me "

"Better take more'n one," Reynolds said. "Meacham, you and Monty Owens ride with him "

Hatfield did not dare protest He neck-reined Goldy as Meacham and Owens left the group and ranged up beside him Owens was a lanky, red-headed man whose leathery cheeks bulged with tobacco

The three rode toward the farms, Meacham loosening the sixes in his low-tied holsters Owens pulled his hat brim low and looked ahead, lynx-eyed, at the farms. Hatfield had hoped to have Meacham alone, but now Owens stacked the odds against him The Ranger had no doubt that both were fast with their sixes, killers, treacherous snakes

Steadily they lengthened the distance between themselves and the fencing crew Matos Creek took a wide bend and the bushes and cottonwoods cut them from sight Twice they saw farmers working in the fields, and the farmers saw them

The men stopped their work, watched them suspiciously, then started on a run toward the village

"They shore figger somethin's up," Meacham laughed, and stroked his holster "Hope they put up a good fight. I ain't had one in a long time."

"Yuh never know when one will come along," Hatfield commented

When they reached the point downstream where the farms ended, Hatfield led the way across the creek and started back up the other side, swinging far out to circle the fields By now Reynolds and the AX crews were directly across creek from him The AX would have to make the wide circle around the farms to reach him in case of trouble, for the nesters would stand as a fighting barrier

Hatfield reached inside his shirt and pulled out his Ranger badge He pinned it over his left pocket Meacham and Owens, keeping a close watch on the farms, paid no attention. The Ranger smiled grimly, continued on for nearly a mile.

He pulled up, quietly sitting his horse. Meacham and Owens reined in, still watching the farms

"If them nesters are goin' to start trouble," Meacham said, "we ought to be ready to help Reynolds. Of course they might come our—"

He turned his head to grin at Hatfield, caught the glint of metal on the man's shirt. His words broke off and his eyes slowly widened The smile remained frozen to his thin lips and he seemed unable to move, paralyzed by sheer surprise. Owens sensed something wrong and jerked his head around.

"Ranger!" Meacham gasped.

"Yuh're under arrest, Meacham and Owens Yuh're charged with murder, accessory to murder and rustlin'. Comin' peaceful?"

Hatfield had made no move toward his guns Rangers always gave the lawbreaker a chance to surrender, even though it often endangered the life of the Ranger himself. The choice of surrender or gunsmoke was left squarely up to the arrested man

Meacham and Owens stared at Hatfield as though they had suddenly come upon a ghost His cold eyes locked with theirs His hands hung easily to either side, and Goldy's reins were dropped loosely over the saddle-horn

"All this time!" Meacham whispered. "All this time, and we never knew!"

CHAPTER XVII

Honest Confession

Suddenly Meacham's eyes narrowed and at the same instant his hands blurred down to his guns Owens' hands slashed savagely for his Colts Hatfield had only a breath of warning A pressure of his knee whirled Goldy around The blue steel Colts fairly jumped from leather

Meacham's slug whipped by his shoulder Owens yelled, streaking to one side to catch Hatfield in a crossfire. The Ranger's Colt blasted and his slug smashed into Meacham's shoulder, driving the man out of saddle Owens' slug whipped off Hatfield's hat and the second burned a hot brand across the Ranger's arm. Hatfield's Colts yammered into the billowing, blinding dust kicked up by the horses' hoofs

Suddenly Owens straightened spasmodically and his guns dropped to the ground. He grabbed for the saddlehorn, clung tightly, his head hanging low Slowly then he slumped to one side and fell in slow motion from saddle His spur caught in the stirrup and the prancing, pirouetting horse dragged him until Hatfield rode alongside and grabbed the bridle He bent down and released the spur. Owen's leg fell like a lifeless log.

A slug whipped across Goldy's withers and plowed a deep furrow in Owens' saddle Hatfield wheeled around Meacham had recovered his six, dragging himself to it Even as Hatfield turned, the renegade lifted the six for a second shot Hatfield's twin Colts lined down.

"Don't try it!" the Ranger snapped

His lips thinned grimly Meacham caught that slight signal, dropped his six and glared, blood streaming from his shoulder

"You win, Ranger," he said thickly. Without warning he toppled to one side, his legs slowly straightening

Hatfield swung out of leather, holstering his Colts. He

bent over Meacham and saw that the man had passed out from loss of blood and the shock of his shoulder wound Hatfield's slug had smashed the bone, and the renegade would not use his right arm for a long time if ever.

Hatfield threw a quick, searching glance at Owens' sprawled body The man was dead, his chest smashed by Ranger lead Hatfield began binding up Meacham's wound He wanted the man alive and able to talk

Hatfield had nearly finished when a slight sound made him stiffen His hand dropped to his holster. A cold voice called a swift and deadly warning

"Yuh won't make it—and live"

Hatfield froze, taloned fingers quivering just above his Colts He was caught in an awkward position, crouched over Meacham, his back to the unknown menace. He felt the skin crawl along his neck and fully expected to feel the smashing impact of tearing lead His chances seemed practically non-existent

A step sounded soft in the grass behind him and rough hands jerked his Colts out of their holsters as a gun muzzle was jabbed hard into his side

"Stand up, and turn around slow," the cold voice ordered

Hatfield slowly came to his feet and turned He faced three farmers One of them held his Colts while the other two covered him with steady rifles One shirt-sleeve was blood-stained where Owen's slug had burned

The badge on Hatfield's shirt caught the glint of the sun. The farmers stared at it

"Texas Ranger!" one of them said softly.

"Yuh sidin' the AX, like Kemper does?" another asked sharply.

"The Rangers side nothin' but the law," Hatfield answered steadily

"This wounded gent rides for the AX," the third farmer said "Reckon the dead hombre did, too"

"They resisted arrest," Hatfield explained. "The wounded one is my prisoner. I want him for murder and rustlin'"

The rifles still covered Hatfield but some of the grim

determination had left the farmers' faces. They exchanged swift glances.

"We'll take you and yore prisoners to the village," one of them said.

"That was in my mind" Hatfield smiled, and all the stern harshness left his lean, tanned face.

"We saw the AX crew comin' our way," tht farmer who had Hatfield's Colts said, almost apologetically. "We heard gunfire and figgered some of our own was in trouble. Hope yuh don't mind, Ranger, if I keep these until we can be real shore of yuh."

"I don't mind," Hatfield said, "but let's get to yore village Reynolds and the AX gunslammers heard the shots, too They'll be burnin' leather to find out what it's all about"

His warning was sufficient. Meacham was placed across his horse and Hatfield mounted Goldy. They let Owens lay, and the renegade's horse trotted aimlessly off across the plain Reynolds would be a mighty puzzled man when he found Owens' body.

It suited Hatfield for the AX to remain in the dark a while longer Reynolds might believe that the nesters had bushwhacked the three AX riders, killing Owens taking Meacham and Geary prisoners. In any case, Hatfield would have plenty of time to cross-examine Meacham in the farmers' settlement AX was not likely to interrupt soon

Hatfield rode across the fields with the men, forded Matos Creek and approached the village Armed men were in the street, ready for any trouble that might come their way On sight of their friends and their prisoners, the farmers flocked to the creek bank. Bob Logsdon pushed through the group

"Geary!" he called "Glad to see yuh."

"The name," the Ranger said with a wide smile, "is Jim Hatfield. Geary was to fool the AX. Tell yore friends I'd like to have my sixes back."

Bob spoke to the farmer who instantly returned the Ranger's guns Meacham was carried into the little store and stretched out on the floor of a bare room in the back. Hatfield grimly looked down at the unconscious man

"Bob," he said to young Logsdon, "I'm goin' to question this man when he comes around. I want you and two or three others to listen. I'd like for Tidy Hart to be present too"

"I'll get Tidy," Bob said, and hurried out

Hatfield cleared the door of the curious farmers and closed it He waited until Bob returned with Tidy and the three farmers who had caught the Ranger bending over Meacham Hatfield shook hands with Tidy.

"The game's about up," he said "Meacham here is the first wolf caught in the trap. I want yuh to listen to him. I reckon it'll clear up a heap of things."

Meacham moaned, and Hatfield signaled the farmers back to the wall He himself leaned against the door Meacham moaned again and his eyes flickered open For a moment he stared up at the ceiling and his forehead creased in a puzzled frown He explored the bandages on his shoulder, pulled himself up, and for the first time realized that he was not alone His eyes circled the silent, waiting men, rested on Hatfield. His lips curled in contempt

"Well, lawdog, what's next?"

"That's up to you," Hatfield replied, without moving "I think yuh got a heap of things to say"

"Not me," Meacham answered. He glanced at the farmers, raised an eyebrow at Tidy Hart "Think these nesters can hold me for long? Kemper'll release me so blamed quick it'll make yore head swim"

No one answered, and Meacham's triumphant words fell flat Once more he looked around the silent ring The light died out of his eyes and his jaw set stubbornly. Then Hatfield spoke quietly and evenly.

"Yuh're not Kemper's prisoner. Yuh forgot a sheriff didn't arrest yuh, but a Ranger did. This is one time yuh face a hangnoose and nobody can help yuh but yoreself"

"Think Matthews—" Meacham started, but Hatfield cut in coldly

"Matthews will have his own neck to worry about. He'll be with yuh in the same jail, Meacham. So will Reynolds Yuh've reached the end of the trail, amigo, and the last card's been played in yore game. I can't promise yuh anything, but I know a court might be more lenient if 'yore information helped bring the others to justice"

Meacham came painfully to his feet and winced as his wounded shoulder throbbed. The air of bravado he tried to assume didn't set well with his shifty eyes

"Yuh can't prove anything," he said defiantly. "Why should I put my own neck in a noose?"

"That's right Everything yuh say will be used against yuh." Hatfield nodded "But I'll remind yuh that I heard yuh say yuh killed Kelly, the AX hoss wrangler. I've heard yuh boast of the times yuh run AX cattle toward Palo Duro Yuh held a six on me and let Lanky Reynolds gun down Ray Logsdon in cold blood."

Meacham stared, and Hatfield went on inexorably:

"Yuh might also know that I've got proof of Deacon Matthews' guilt in his own handwritin' and the list includes yore name I aim to arrest every gunslammer on the AX payroll Yuh don't think they'll all keep their mouths shut, do yuh? Yuh better tell the truth yoreself before somebody else tells it and yuh lose yore chance for the court's mercy"

A pallor of fear spread over Meacham's pinched face. He looked like a trapped rat. Unconsciously he touched his throat as if he could already feel the hempen noose around it.

"What d'yuh want to know?" he choked hoarsely.

"Who stole AX beefs? How many times did yuh have a hand in it?" Hatfield paused impressively "With Matthews' record, Meacham, yuh'll only confirm what I already know I want these gents to hear it"

"I—Reynolds' bunch stole every head of beef that turned up missin'," Meacham said, in a swift rush of words "They was stole over the last year and a half I reckon I've been on almost every drive we made to Palo Duro"

"Why was the farmers blamed?"

"Because Matthews figgered that would throw the owners and everybody else off our trail Folks knew the AX had trouble with Matos Creek and figgered the AX wouldn't steal from itself."

"How about killin's on the AX?" Hatfield shot at him.

"Tidy had his own bunch and Matthews couldn't do nothin' with 'em. So they had to be replaced with Reynolds' boys Every time a man was killed, it'd scare the others that much more."

"He's right," Tidy spoke up. "Some of my punchers asked for their time after each shootin'. Most of 'em stuck though"

"Brant Trimpe," Hatfield said suddenly "Who killed him, and why?"

"He'd have made a dicker with the farmers and the game would have been over," Meacham answered. "We had to keep 'em stirred up."

"Who did the job?"

"Deacon Matthews. Leastways, I heard Lanky say the Deacon done it "

"How about Stumpy Calvert?"

"Lanky did that killin' hisself I was with him."

"One more question, Meacham. Where does Matthews bank the dinero made from the stolen cows?"

"Childress," Meacham answered. "He has the buyers deposit to his favor Deacon splits up the take among the rest of us Kemper puts his dinero right in the Matos Bank "

Hatfield looked around at the silent farmers.

"Yuh've been witnesses to this man's statements. Yuh'll be called on to repeat 'em in court. Yuh know how yuh been used as a cover for a big cattle steal and how murders have been blamed on yuh. Yuh know why "

"Makes me boil," Bob Logsdon gritted. He turned to Meacham "Why did Reynolds gun for my pa?"

"Because Matthews figgered it would suit his plans better if yuh was disorganized, suspicious of one another and fighting among yoreselves. Yuh're slated for Boot Hill, too, Logsdon—for the same reason."

Suddenly someone pounded loudly on the door Hatfield unlocked it, hand dropping to his six An excited man burst in

"Bob, AX is fencing us in! They've done got a heap of wire up! We won't be able to get off Matos Creek if they finish it "

Young Logsdon swore and the rest of the men pushed toward the door Jim Hatfield blocked their passage, his eyes cold.

"What yuh aim to do?" he demanded.

"Blast that wire and the AX gun crew plumb out of Texas!" Bob answered angrily

Hatfield's smile was crooked "That's exactly what Matthews expects yuh to do Yuh're settin' tight right here till I give yuh the signal"

"We can't be cut off from Matos," a farmer disagreed.

"Yuh won't be," Hatfield promised "I want time to make a few more arrests I'm arrestin' Kemper and Matthews How much fight do yuh think'll be left in Reynolds then?"

"Not much," Bob admitted He looked sharply at the Ranger. "Ain't yuh puttin' yore own neck out?"

"Mebbe," Hatfield snapped, "but it has to be done. Tidy, in case of trouble I think you and Miss Hart better leave the village and head for Matos."

"I'm not runnin'," Tidy bristled "I been wantin' a chance at Matthews"

"Yuh'll get it! But first see yore daughter's safe from that bunch of sidewinders I'll meet yuh in Matos" Hatfield added grimly, "I reckon yuh'll eat plenty of gunsmoke after that"

CHAPTER XVIII

Open War

Ben Meacham was securely locked in a tight little tool shed, where there was little chance that the AX gun crew could rescue him Hatfield sent Tidy scurrying away to get his daughter and prepare for a long circuitous drive to Matos Hatfield intended to have that town well cleaned up before the Harts arrived.

He held a brief conference with Bob, suggesting the farmers make a quick scout of the new fence that was being built This would keep Lanky Reynolds' attention on the farmers, giving Tidy a chance to get away, and the Ranger the opportunity to work with a free hand in Matos Tidy still grumbled about riding off, but saw the wisdom of the move because of his daughter

Hatfield waited until a group of farmers left the village, headed toward the fence The Ranger judged that Reynolds would call in his gunhawks when he sighted this party. When Hatfield was certain that the coast was clear, he started Tidy and Clarice on their way Then he had a few last words with Bob Logsdon, swung into saddle and rode off himself.

Hatfield made a huge circle far to the north of the farms along the creek When he forded the stream at last and headed toward Matos he kept an alert watch for riders, but there were none The AX was concentrating on the fence along Matos Creek.

At last Matos came into sight Hatfield reined in and studied the town, then approached Matos from the south, coming in at the rear of the buildings and the cottonwood behind the jail Not far off stood the tree beneath which the evidence against Deacon Matthews rested

Hatfield dismounted, dropped the reins over Goldy's head, strode around the jail and paused on the plank sidewalk. No one noticed the slim Ranger whose alert eyes cut quickly up and down the street. Satisfied that as yet the town had no news from the AX, Hatfield turned into the sheriff's office

Kemper was not behind his desk or in the cell block. Hatfield left the office, going directly to the bank The cashier behind the grilled window looked surprised and a bit frightened when he saw the star on Hatfield's broad chest. He quickly answered the Ranger's questions, and Meacham's story about Kemper's deposits was confirmed. Hatfield's eyes locked with those of the cashier.

"Yuh'd know Kemper didn't make near that much money as law officer," he said "Didn't yuh wonder about that?"

"Of course," the man replied. "But what could we do? Since all those gunhawks came to the AX, it hasn't been healthy to talk about Kemper, Matthews or any of them. Who would arrest Kemper? Kemper, himself? He's the only lawman in these parts "

Hatfield ordered the lawman's account frozen and the records put in a safe place That done, he left the bank and returned to the sheriff's office.

He pushed through the door and Kemper looked up from his desk The sheriff grinned and turned his attention again to the open desk drawer through which he was rumaging Then something seemed to dawn on the man His groping hand became still and he slowly raised his head. His eyes centered on the Ranger badge, lifted disbelievingly to the grim face above it

"You!" he exclaimed He came slowly to his feet. "But yuh're—Reynolds hired yuh. I don't savvy."

"The game's finished, Kemper," Hatfield said quietly. "Yuh're under arrest for malfeasance in office, accesory to murder and rustlin' Hand over yore badge "

Kemper gulped, seemed unable to move. Hatfield waited, hands hanging loose at his side The next move was up to the crooked lawman

Kemper found his voice "Yuh can't pin nothing like that on me. I've done the best I could in this job!"

"Yuh forget I was along when yuh investigated a murder and a rustlin' Yuh was deliberately blind to a heap of sign Whatever Reynolds or Matthews said, you did. The law and its protection is for everybody, Kemper, not for just one or two men I've just come from the bank where I had a look at yore savin's. There's a heap of dinero comin' from nowhere Yuh can explain that to a court, if yuh can Hand over yore badge."

Kemper slowly unpinned the star. Hatfield was glad that the man intended to give up peacefully. Kemper moved away from the desk and carefully unbuckled his gunbelt, swinging it to the desk.

"Unlock a cell," Hatfield said flatly.

Kemper stubbornly shook his head "I've give up my badge and dropped my six. Blamed if I'm goin' to lock myself in my own cell That's yore job."

He reached in his pocket and threw the heavy keys on the desk. Hatfield picked them up, nodded toward the cell block. Beyond the door was a narrow barred corridor, two cells opening from either side They were empty at the moment Kemper marched to the end of the corridor, stopped and turned. Hatfield inserted the key in the lock and swung the barred door.

At that instant Kemper struck, throwing his heavy body on the Ranger, swinging a punch toward Hatfield's face The blow caught Hatfield alongside the jaw and slammed him back against the bars His head struck the steel and a wave of dizziness swept over him.

Kemper made a wild grab for one of Hatfield's Colts, jerked it from holster The man had craftily planned his escape attempt. He had not dared try to match the Ranger's gun speed, but here in the corridor, Hatfield could not avoid his rush, and surprise was the renegade lawman's ally

As Hatfield felt the Colt jerked from holster his hand dropped to snatch out the other one. Kemper swung the weapon down and the muzzle raked across Hatfield's forehead. The Ranger went sprawling to the floor, brain spinning, every muscle flaccid. Kemper raced down the corridor

"Halt!" Hatfield called

Suddenly Kemper wheeled, the six streaking up and

lining toward Hatfield. The Ranger's own six swept up even as he looked into the black muzzle of the gun Kemper held Both weapons roared almost as one Kemper's slug struck a bar just above Hatfield's head, sang off in a shrill ricochet.

Kemper came up on his toes as Hatfield's slug hit him. He dropped the gun, turned heavily, and took a step toward the door, arm held out blindly before him He took a second step, shuddered and suddenly collapsed, half-in and half-out of the doorway.

Hatfield came to his feet His head felt as if it had split open and there was the warm touch of blood along his forehead and down one cheek. His head had cleared a little, though, and the ringing had left his ears

He moved to Kemper's slack form and bent down The lawman was dead.

The Ranger retrieved the gun Kemper had snatched, and walked into the office He staunched the flow of blood and cleaned the wound with water from a drinking pail That done, he ejected the empties from his sixes, reloaded, and stepped out the door. Men stood on the canopied store porches and in the street, looking toward the jail. Hatfield's badge caught the sun, a silent challenge to any of Matthews' men who might be around.

At last Hatfield started toward the bank, walking in long strides, his spurs jingling, his arms swinging rhythmically so that his hands brushed his holsters No one moved. People silently watched the lithe figure that represented the power of the law of the State of Texas.

Hatfield turned in at the bank building His fingers taloned slightly as he stepped in the door and stood at the foot of the steep stairway There was no challenge, no sound. Hatfield mounted the steps until his eyes cleared the top, and he could look down the hall. Matthews' door was closed.

Hatfield loosened the Colts and strode to the door. He knocked, turned the knob and entered, muscles tensed for instant action. No one was in the office and it looked undisturbed. Hatfield placed his hand on the leather seat of the swivel chair. It was faintly warm. Matthews had been here not long before.

His face grim, eyes cold, Hatfield strode out of the office and down to the street He saw the bank cashier watching him curiously.

"Seen Matthews?" Hatfield called.

"He came into the bank right after you left," the man called back "He asked some questions about you, but I evaded them."

"Where'd he go?"

"Headed toward his home," the cashier answered.

Hatfield knew that the crooked ranch manager had seen the Ranger walk from the jail to the bank and back again. From his office window Matthews must have seen the law badge on the shirt of a man he believed to be a gunhawk. Matthews had quickly sensed the truth.

Hatfield silently cursed himself. If he had waited for Kemper at the jail, he might have caught both men. But regrets were of no use.

Hatfield hurried to Goldy and swung into saddle. The golden sorrel streaked around the corner of the jail and galloped toward Matthews' home.

The house was a low, rambling building shaded by a few trees It looked deserted but the Ranger, from experience, did not trust appearances.

He vaulted from saddle and ran at a tense crouch up the walk.

Crossing the porch he kicked open the door and wheeled to one side out of line of any gunfire.

There was no sound and the house echoed hollowly. Hatfield stepped into the front room, Colts ready.

He saw no one, crossed the room, and edged through another door. From here he could see into the bedroom which looked as if a cyclone had torn through it Dresser drawers stood open, with articles of clothing hanging from them. Someone had ripped aside the bed covers, getting something out from under the mattress. A box of shells stood open on a marble-topped washstand, more than half of its contents gone

Hatfield looked at the destruction, then moved to the back of the house and out to the barn.

Matthews' buggy stood in the runway but his horse was gone.

Apparently Matthews had made his escape from Matos.

Hatfield tried to determine in which direction the man would flee The railroad to the east offered the swiftest way out of the country.

But Matthews would be running directly away from his ill-gotten money

The AX was close by, but Matthews must have guessed it would offer only temporary refuge Yet he would also know that he could use the gunhawks for protection in his flight.

And it lay directly on the shortest road to the distant Border.

CHAPTER XIX

Prisoners on the AX

Quickly Jim Hatfield swung into saddle and rode back to the main street He stopped before the sheriff's office where a curious crowd had gathered They caught sight of him and turned, silent and curious

"Kemper," Hatfield said, "resisted arrest. Yuh can guess it has somethin' to do with the AX and the renegades out there Matos has no lawman till yuh can elect one." His cold eyes rested on a middle-aged man with a strong jaw and a direct, open look. "What's yore handle."

"Abe Simon."

"I hereby appoint yuh as my deputy, Simon, to assume the duties of the local law officer till an election can be held Pin Kemper's star on yore shirt. I reckon yuh'll keep Matos a heap cleaner'n he did "

Hatfield neck-reined Goldy and rode out of town at a fast gallop. He headed directly for the AX spread, hoping against hope to catch up with Matthews before the man reached his renegade allies.

Several miles out, Hatfield suddenly drew rein. He stiffened, staring at a wrecked buckboard on the side of the road. One wheel had been broken The sides were scarred with bullets Hatfield grimly examined the vehicle from the saddle,

It told a mute story Tidy Hart and Clarice had circled far to the south until they had reached this point, and here they had run into trouble. From the number of bullet scars, Hatfield judged that several riders had attacked the buckboard.

The Ranger was sure that Tidy and Clarice were not dead, for the renegades would not have bothered to carry the bodies off Father and daughter were prisoners —on the AX There could be no other answer to the signs of destruction.

117

Grimly the Ranger wheeled Goldy around. There was no further need to trail Matthews. He had met his gunhawk companions. Hatfield rode toward the farms along Matos Creek. From the nesters he could gather a fighting force of tremendous power.

It was open war But Hatfield grimly intended to make it a short one.

He made a wide circuit of the AX and came into the village from the far side of the creek At first appearance it looked peaceful but Hatfield had already been stopped by alert farmers who looked ready for any kind of trouble. The moment he had forded the creek and came into the single street, Bob Logsdon came hurrying out of the general store.

"Everything quiet," the young man reported "I've got men watchin' that fence, and Reynolds is mighty busy watchin' us I think he expects trouble Meacham's safe enough."

Hatfield swung out of leather.

"Kemper resisted arrest," he said, "and he's dead. Matthews made a run for it and headed for the AX. He's there now. But I got bad news Tidy and Miss Hart was caught by those renegades."

"Caught!" Bob paled. He grabbed Hatfield's arm. "Not —hurt?"

"They ain't dead, if that's what yuh mean," Hatfield answered. "I hope they're not hurt But Matthews has 'em on the AX He and Reynolds know their game's up, and I figger they'll try to use Tidy and Miss Hart as hostages, so's they can make their escape."

"Matthews and Reynolds are cold-blooded snakes," Bob answered tightly, "and they never liked Tidy. He bucked 'em too hard. Reynolds always was sort of sweet on Clarice, though she shore let him know he wasn't wanted Can yuh figger what might happen?"

"I can," Hatfield answered. "Get yore boys together— pronto"

In a short time most of the farmers crowded around the store A few of them remained to watch the AX crew at the line of fence posts Hatfield mounted a wooden

118

box and spread his hands wide for silence. He briefly outlined what had happened

"Every manjack of the AX crew is subject to arrest," he said "They're rustlers and some of 'em are killers. I can't round up the whole bunch alone, therefore I appoint yuh as my deputies We're goin' to clean up the AX so's the rightful owners will have control of it again That means yuh'll get a square deal and, if yuh sell, a fair price for yore land"

"Let's start!" someone in the crowd yelled, and Hatfield jumped down off the box.

He and Bob Logsdon led the way toward the far edge of the fields beyond the fringe of bushes that lined the creek. Behind them came the armed farmers, eager to strike back at the renegades who had harmed them in so many ways.

The AX had set up many more posts Wire had already been stretched for a short distance, and AX gunhawks covered the workers, keeping a wary eye on the line of men who watched them just out of six-gun range.

When the new crowd of men came, the AX men instantly bunched for a swift conference, then began spreading out The workers dropped their tools and joined the fighters Hatfield walked steadily on. He halted in due time.

"I'm a Texas Ranger!" he called to the renegades "I'm orderin' yuh here and now to lay down yore sixes and surrender. Yuh're charged with rustlin'. If any of yuh are innocent, yuh'll have a chance to prove it in court"

"Yuh're a doublecrossin' snake, Geary!" a man yelled back "If yuh want us, come and get us!"

"Yuh still got a chance," Hatfield told them "Yuh can surrender peaceful and nobody will get hurt."

His answer was a slug that cut the air close to his cheek. Instantly nester guns answered the challenge. Hatfield dropped flat, both sixes snaking from leather. Bob lay to one side, eyes narrowed over his gunsights. Gun thunder rolled across the wide Texas plain as renegade and nester fought to the showdown.

The farmers downed three of the AX crew on the first.

119

fire, though they lost one of their own men. Slugs whipped through the grass and whined through the air just above Hatfield's head. His sixes smashed and roared at anything that moved ahead of him. He caught one killer directly between the eyes Another of his slugs smashed a renegade's leg. The man threshed and moaned in the high grass.

The farmers made a swift advance, but the cold fury of the renegade fire drove them to cover And they were wasting precious time. Matthews would be moving fast to escape and Reynolds was not with the men who were defending the AX wire.

Hatfield emptied his gun, ejected the spent shells and reloaded He caught Bob Logsdon's eye and signaled the young man to follow him They crawled through the grass, bullets constantly whipping above them Suddenly some of the slugs began to thud into the ground around Hatfield He caught a movement in the grass to his right. Instantly his slugs were searching in the matted grass.

A man jerked upright, eyes staring in stunned amazement. He coughed, then fell forward on his face Hatfield and Bob Logsdon continued to crawl away from the fight

"Yore boys can handle the fracas here, Hatfield told Bob "This fight is givin' Matthews and Reynolds time to get away, mebbe with Tidy and Miss Hart Yuh game to tackle the ranch?"

"Any time yuh say," Bob answered promptly.

Hatfield smiled, grimness suddenly leaving his face The young farmer was living up to the Ranger's estimate of his character. He was a good man to have as a partner in tight

"We'll get our horses," Hatfield said, "and burn leather to the AX Mebbe we'll get there in time."

"We'd better!" Bob gritted.

They left the farmers slowly pushing the renegades back The gunhawks put up a good fight, but the farmers were paying them back in their own coin, and the Ranger had no doubt of the outcome The renegades would break and scatter Many would escape the law this time. But with Kemper dead and Meacham held,

Hatfield would be content to round up Matthews and Reynolds They were the real culprits.

In the village the Ranger and Bob Logsdon stopped at the store long enough to fill their pockets with shells, then vaulted into the saddle They sped off down the street, splashed across Matos Creek, and streaked across the fields

They made a wide circuit of the battling renegades and raced toward the AX spread. They went straight as an arrow for their goal until they saw the trees of the AX far ahead Bob Logsdon slowed up and Hatfield reined Goldy around.

"We'd better figger some way of gettin' in there without gettin' ourselves filled with holes," Bob said

"Boldness will do it," Hatfield declared "If Matthews and Reynolds are still there they won't expect me or you to be ridin' in from this direction Their gunslammers will be holdin' up the farmers I'm supposed to be in Matos, or comin' from town "

"How yuh figger to ride in?" Bob demanded

"We'll go streakin' right toward the place and into the yard," Hatfield said. "They'll figger we're bringin' news from the creek If we keep our heads down and our hats low, we can be in the yard before they know different."

"Then what?" Bob asked

"We can play the cards as they fall."

"Yuh sound like a gambler, Hatfield, not a Ranger," Bob answered as he grinned

"I've been both " Hatfield laughed. "There's times yuh have to gamble when yuh wear the law badge "

Bob pulled his hat brim low and streaked after the Ranger when Hatfield set Goldy at a dead run toward the ranch As they neared, at first Hatfield thought the buildings were deserted Then he saw two men run out into the yard and a third joined them They stared toward the approaching riders, then hurried toward the yard gate

Hatfield raised his arm and waved as he raced along, as though he were coming with important news Hatfield was beginning to think he and Bob were going to get away with the trick when one of the men in the yard suddenly yelled and pointed toward the golden sorrel "Geary! It's that Ranger who fooled us! They ain't our boys!"

Instantly the three men went for their guns By now Hatfield and Logsdon were fairly close Hatfield jerked erect, his hands slashed down, and the heavy Colts blurred up even as the renegades made a desperate play for their own weapons.

Logsdon wheeled away from Hatfield and his six met the renegades' fire Hatfield headed straight for the gate Bullets sang around him but he thundered down on the gunhawks One of them spun half-around and dropped like an empty sack. Logsdon's slug caught a second, knocking his leg out from under him. The third one slammed a bullet at Hatfield, missed by a hair's breadth And the Ranger's slug crashed into his temple

Hatfield didn't slacken his speed, but headed for the ranchhouse. He and Logsdon came to a sliding halt and vaulted from saddle Colts in their hands, hammers dogged back, they raced for the wide veranda The Ranger was worried If Reynolds and Matthews were here, they would surely have disclosed their presence by now

Ranger and farmer hit the porch together, plunged for the door Hatfield's broad shoulder smashed it back against the wall and he catapulted into the kitchen He saw no one, hurried to the next room, found it empty

"Gone! They've slipped through our fingers!"

Bob Logsdon swore, and there was fright in his eyes Too vividly he could imagine Clarice in Reynolds' clutches Hatfield's jaw tightened.

Suddenly he stiffened, catching the sound of a racing vehicle He jumped to the window A buckboard had wheeled out of the barn and was tearing for the yard gate Matthews sat in the seat, his whip cracking over the team The Ranger glimpsed two roped forms lying in the back Reynolds, on a powerful bay, was just behind the speeding vehicle. The killers had a head start!

CHAPTER XX

Flight

Grimly Hatfield realized that their quarry had waited quietly in the barn, team hitched, their hostages bound and loaded in the buckboard The sudden appearance of the Ranger and his partner had interrupted their escape. So they had delayed until the moment the Ranger and Logsdon had disappeared into the house Then they made their bid for freedom

Hatfield smashed the glass with his gun barrel and fired at the fleeing renegades Reynolds twisted around in saddle but neither he nor Matthews slackened speed Hatfield and Bob rushed outside and ran for their horses, hurtling into saddle

By now the buckboard was speeding across the grassy plain Hatfield and Logsdon thundered out of the yard in hot pursuit Goldy quickly outstripped Logsdon's horse and lessened the distance between the Ranger and his quarry Reynolds threw swift glances over his shoulder, seemed to be judging Hatfield's distance Matthews headed in a direction which would take him several miles away from where his men were battling the deputized farmers.

Reynolds suddenly bent down and swept a rifle out of the saddle-boot He twisted around and the rifle jumped to his shoulder Hatfield was beyond six-gun range. He instantly threw himself low over Goldie's head and jerked the horse to one side The rifle cracked and the bullet whined where Hatfield had been a breath before. Reynolds levered a second shell in the chamber.

"Keep yore distance!" he yelled

He set spurs to his horse and raced after the buckboard

The rifle gave the renegades a tremendous advantage, and the Ranger realized it. He and Bob Logsdon would make easy targets before they could get close enough for their sixes to be effective As yet, the terrific pace continued but Hatfield knew that sooner or later it would settle down to a grim and deadly flight It was then that he expected Matthews to put his hostages to use •

At the moment, Hatfield could do little more than press hard upon the renegades Goldy had an immense amount of stamina and could outlast the renegades' horses

The hard, pounding pace went on for several miles Hatfield would press close until Reynolds would use the rifle, then he would drop back. Gradually the buckboard slowed. Hatfield reined in Goldy, and Bob came alongside

"I'm makin' a wide circle around 'em," Hatfield said "Reynolds will try to stop me with that rifle When he turns toward me, you come in from this side Fade back when he lines yuh in his sights and I'll ride in."

"Wear him down?" Bob demanded

"Partly that" Hatfield nodded "But if I can work over beyond 'em, I can start heading 'em toward Matos Creek. I figger mebbe some of yore friends can take a hand."

"How about Clarice—and Tidy?"

"They'll be used to protect them snakes somehow. Don't know yet"

Hatfield set spurs to Goldy and cut away from Bob at a sharp angle. The buckboard team trotted on, Reynolds close to the buckboard conferring with Matthews Reynolds saw Hatfield's move and instantly maneuvered to intercept him Bob Logsdon as instantly dashed for the buckboard, and Matthews' yell warned Reynolds The gunhawk rode back and Hatfield continued his wide circuit, finally placing himself directly across the line of escape

He edged in closer and Reynolds moved to meet the threat - Bob Logsdon closed the distance Matthews stopped the buckboard, spoke briefly to Reynolds He stood up and cupped his hands, yelling to Hatfield

"Better let us alone, Ranger! We got Tidy and his girl here Yuh wouldn't want 'em to get hurt"

"I'm callin' on you and Reynolds to surrender!"

Hatfield called back "If yuh harm the Harts, yuh place that much more trouble on yoreself"

"We'll decide that," Matthews cried "You can't get near us, Hatfield You can't make your arrest"

"Yore case is hopeless," Hatfield yelled. "We got yuh bracketed"

The two renegades conferred for awhile Reynolds pointed to the roped forms in the back of the buckboard

Suddenly Hatfield knew what they planned and it sent a cold chill down his back Reynolds must have suggested that Matthews forget the hostages and the buckboard Using one of the horses as a mount, and relieved of Tidy and Clarice, the two renegades would make a dash for it They could ride down Hatfield before Bob Logsdon could close with them

The Ranger touched spurs to Goldy's flanks and the sorrel sprang forward Hatfield's sixes were lifted, but he held his fire Instantly Reynolds' rifle came up

Reynolds fired, and the rifle bullet came close. The renegade worked the lever, and Hatfield was a little closer. He still held his own fire until he could be sure that his slugs would reach the target

Reynolds leveled the rifle again Matthews yelled and grabbed his partner. The rifle barrel jumped up as Reynolds fired Matthews pointed toward Bob Logsdon who was rushing in from the other side For a moment, Reynolds was uncertain, looking first one way, then the other. Hatfield urged Goldy to greater speed He was in pistol range now, and rapidly closing the gap

Deacon Matthews suddenly jumped over the seat of the buckboard and jerked his six free of leather Hatfield pulled Goldy to a sliding halt. Reynolds lifted his rifle, but Hatfield centered his guns on Matthews as the man bent over the forms in the buckboard Hatfield dropped the hammers.

Matthews screamed and fell out of the buckboard. Reynolds fired, the bullet smashing into Hatfield's shoulder The Ranger grabbed for the saddle-horn, missed and tumbled from the sorrel He dimly heard Bob Logsdon yell

Hatfield pulled himself to his knees, groped for his

125

fallen six that lay in the grass. He shook his head to clear his spinning brain, looked up. Logsdon was down, his horse threshing wildly on the ground.

Reynolds wheeled and came rushing toward Hatfield, seeing his way clear to freedom Hatfield slowly lifted the six, biting his lips against the waves of pain that swept over him As Reynolds loomed closer, Hatfield could see the cruel lips peeled back from the teeth in an ugly grimace The renegade had abandoned the rifle and clutched a heavy six It lined down on the Ranger as Hatfield lifted his own Colt

The gun thunder of the two weapons blended. Hatfield felt the whip of the wind as the bullet cut by his ear Reynolds fell backward over the cantle He hit the ground and rolled loosely, ending in a huddled heap His horse fled over the plain.

Hatfield painfully pulled himself erect. Bob Logsdon came running toward the buckboard and Hatfield stared at him in amazement. The Ranger held onto Goldy while Bob cut the ropes that held Tidy and Clarice Bob held the girl close in his arms a moment, then hurried to Hatfield

"Thought yuh was killed," the Ranger said heavily. Bob smiled

"Reynolds killed my hoss and I was thrown Hatfield, yore shootin' saved Clarice and Tidy. Matthews aimed to kill 'em."

With Bob's help, Hatfield walked to the buckboard. Matthews lay on the ground, badly wounded Reynolds was dead Tidy looked badly rumpled but otherwise seemed unhurt He immediately started to work on Hatfield's shoulder, with Clarice helping.

"Just a flesh wound," Tidy said, relieved. "Shock and loss of blood makes yuh feel rocky. Reckon all of us owe yuh a heap, Hatfield. We'd almost reached Matos when we run into Reynolds and three of his boys. They captured us just when Matthews came up He said yuh'd split things wide open in Matos. Him and Reynolds decided to run for it, usin' us as hostages You come along too soon and killed the three gunhawks. I reckon yuh know the rest."

Hatfield nodded When his wound was bandaged, Bob and Tidy helped him up on Goldy Matthews was patched up as well as possible and loaded into the buckboard beside Reynolds' body.

Bob took the reins, turned the team toward Matos Creek Hatfield followed, face hard set against the pain of his shoulder.

When they reached Matos Creek, the fight there was over Hatfield knew that this case was broken Meacham's testimony and the ledger account, which he could safely produce now, would stand up in any court The murders on the Matos range were solved Matthews, Meacham and the captured renegades would pay for them by the hangnoose. For Matthews would live to face justice, despite his bad wound Reynolds had already gone to a much higher court than any man on earth could establish.

Bob Logsdon neatly summed it up

"Yuh've freed Matos Range, Hatfield Yuh've given us farmers a chance and restored the AX to the honest, square gents that own it" He flushed, and smiled at Clarice "Yuh worked things around so's Clarice and me can get married, and yuh're to be best man at the weddin' next week"

It took that long to wind up the case. Matthews lay in jail, slowly recovering from his wound, and Meacham occupied the next cell Matthews had completely caved in when he had heard Meacham's evidence and had seen the ledger which Hatfield presented to the new sheriff. He had confessed to the whole crooked scheme of bleeding the AX white Under merciless cross-examination, he broke, confessing that his bullet had ended the life of Brant Trimpe . .

Two weeks later, Hatfield walked into Captain McDowell's office in Austin The old man looked at him, cleared his throat

"Good work, Jim I'm mighty proud of yuh The Rangers have closed another case How's yore shoulder?"

"Fine A little stiff, that's all"

"Reckon it wouldn't bother yuh?"

Hatfield chuckled "Yuh got another case in mind?"

McDowell's eyes blazed and his face suffused with anger His fist thumped down on his desk so that everything jumped.

"There's a bunch of ornery polecats figger they can besmirch the State of Texas! They figger they're smarter'n any Ranger that ever was born! They figger there ain't no law higher'n their own six-guns! It's plumb—"

He paused for breath. Hatfield smiled and stretched out his legs Adventure called again—and he was ready!

www.ingramcontent.com/pod-product-compliance
Lightning Source LLC
Chambersburg PA
CBHW020146180626
46810CB00004B/1764